ONE HUNDRED GOODBYES

AN ASPEN COVE SMALL TOWN ROMANCE

KELLY COLLINS

BOOK NOOK PRESS

CHAPTER ONE

EDEN

Eden Webster sat at her desk looking through the stack of mail. She'd sorted it no less than a dozen times this week. There was the due last week pile, the due this week pile, and the long overdue pile she was certain would send her to debtor's prison any day.

Suzanne said she'd take care of it all, but Suzanne was missing in action. After placing a call each day for the last week to her sister, she'd about given up on connecting.

Her stomach growled and her belly rippled as the baby moved inside her.

She laid her hand on the tight skin of her rounded stomach and waited for the little foot to push against her palm. It seemed to be their game.

Her stomach would growl, and the baby would kick as if telling her to keep it quiet in there.

"Hey little one," she crooned. "How about a peanut butter and jelly sandwich?"

She rolled slowly to her feet. At nearly eight months pregnant, she moved like a sloth. Getting to her feet from a seated position seemed to be almost as challenging as getting out of bed. Though she'd only gained twenty-five pounds, she felt as big as a house.

Porkchop did a figure eight around her ankles, swishing his long tail back and forth as Eden moved to the counter and pulled out the bread and peanut butter.

"It's a good thing you like peanut butter." She stared down at the cat, who sat more like a dog ready to beg. "You're impossible, you know that?"

Porkchop had belonged to her elderly neighbor Grace. When her children moved her into a long-term care home, they'd asked Eden to take the cat.

Sucker must have been written all over her face. If there was a word that wasn't in Eden's vocabulary, it was no.

She glanced down at the cotton stretching over her belly. Her inability to say no had gotten her into this situation in the first place.

She slathered the peanut butter on two slices

of white bread and scraped the grape jelly jar clean.

Looking down at Porkchop, she didn't have the heart not to share, so she tore a corner of her sandwich free and put it on a plate.

She knew the feline well enough to know she'd lift her nose now, but as soon as Eden turned her back, the cat would gobble it down. Porkchop was the opposite of Eden. She always said no initially.

A glance at the clock told Eden it was time to go. She'd been lucky to keep her job at Rocco's Bar and Grill. The work was tough, but the check was helpful when her sister forgot about the promises she'd made, which had happened quite frequently over the last couple of months.

Eden was the pregnant one, but it seemed as if her sister suffered from baby brain.

The cat followed her to the door like she did every afternoon. She reached down to stroke Porkchop's fur. At five, she was still a kitten at heart and flopped to her back to swat at Eden's hand.

"There's no time to play. I have to get to work or you won't be getting any treats this week." At the mention of treats, Porkchop dashed into the kitchen where they were stored. It was the perfect opportunity for Eden to slip on her jacket and leave.

In the hallway, old man Shubert shuffled toward the elevator. "Hold the car will ya, Eden?"

She wanted to groan because holding the car for Mr. Shubert meant she'd have to wait five minutes for him to close the twenty-foot distance.

Instead, she smiled. "No problem." She leaned against the open doors that tried to close constantly. The thumping against her back eased the pinch she felt at her tailbone. "Take your time."

The old man laughed. "Time is all I've got." When he finally arrived, he looked down at her belly. "You look like you're ready to pop."

She shouldered her purse and moved aside so he could enter the elevator. "I've got about six weeks left." Her hands lovingly stroked her stomach.

"Boy or girl?"

He asked her that each time he saw her. The answer was always the same. "It's got to be one or the other, but I don't know which." The sex of the baby was a mystery.

"Where's the father?"

That was always the second question. Eden didn't have a man in her life. She hadn't for quite some time. "He's somewhere out there."

"Better track him down."

She pressed the button for the lobby, and

when the doors opened, she wished Mr. Shubert a good day and walked into the sunshine.

Late summer and fall were her favorite times of the year. The trees in the Rockies would turn into a cornucopia of colors. It wasn't too hot, and the ugly grip of winter was still months away from Denver.

She hopped on the bus and took it downtown. It would have been easier to drive but her doctor wasn't fond of her getting behind the wheel, given that her entire pregnancy was in front of her. Many women gained their weight all around, but Eden was one of those that grew forward. From the back, no one would know she was so far along. It was the basketball up front that gave it all away.

At 16th Street, she exited and walked by her favorite candy store. She had one constant craving. Good & Plenty were certainly good but not always plenty, as few stores carried the pink and white coated candies. Black licorice was a taste at her late stages of pregnancy she required regularly.

Digging through her purse, she found the sixty-three cents she'd need to buy a package.

Sharma smiled as she walked inside. The clerk pulled a pink and white box from under the counter. "I saved this for you."

"You're a saint." She set her change on the

counter, picking out the piece of purse lint that had gotten mixed into the coins.

"No, I'm Punjabi, which is close to being a saint."

Eden raised the box to her lips and kissed it. "Thank you. I'll be able to get through the night with these."

She made her way down the outside mall and walked into work.

One look around told everyone that Rocco's taste in waitresses went to curvy blondes but not pregnant curvy. Rocco looked at her from behind the bar and shook his head. He'd hired her long before she'd decided to have a baby. His look was as dark as the paneling that covered the walls.

An apron sailed through the air toward her and he pointed toward the back of the restaurant. Her evening assignment was no surprise. As soon as she started to show, he hid her.

Eden hung up her coat and grabbed a handful of candies before she went to her station. She had two tables seated with what looked like another on the way. Things would pick up once the dinner crowd hit.

Three hours and sixteen pizzas later, she looked up to find her ex Matt in her corner booth canoodling his girlfriend—a doppelgänger of her-

ONE HUNDRED GOODBYES

self. Blonde hair and brown eyed, she was the spitting image of Eden minus the baby.

Everyone always said people had a type. Matt sure did. By the looks of the new one, he liked them blonde, petite and enamored. Eden had been his type for two years. When things became comfortable, he found himself another. This was number three if her count was correct.

"Welcome to Rocco's." She smiled like she did for everyone, although with Matt it was harder to pin the corners of her lips up. "Can I start you with something to drink?" She looked at Matt, knowing his girlfriend would never get to choose.

"Hey, Eden." His eyes skimmed her body, stopping on her stomach. "You're looking—"

"Oh, my God," Blondie said. "You're huge. How does a person have sex like that?"

Eden smiled and caressed her belly. "Sex?" She stared at Matt. "Never had it. Or at least it wasn't memorable. How about a bottle of Chianti?"

It was almost comical to watch Matt's arrogance wilt. "Chianti sounds great." His eyes never lifted from her stomach. "Who's the father?"

She shrugged her shoulders. "It's hard to tell." Eden turned and walked away.

Matt and his new toy didn't bother her the rest of the night. It was a regular named Dave Mason that was the problem. Each time she leaned over the bar he caressed her backside. There was no point in talking to Rocco because Dave was his best buddy. Served in the army for years together. Eden was smart enough to know that Rocco's motto was bro's before ho's and a ho was anything that didn't have a penis.

She hefted a tray of beers to her shoulders and turned, but not before Dave slid his hand between her legs.

She lost her balance.

She had a choice.

She could save the beers and fall into Dave's lap or she could drop the tray and step aside. She chose option two and the tray of mugs went crashing to the floor.

"Dammit, Eden. What the hell happened?"

Eden looked around to make sure no one was hurt. Except for a sprinkling of lager on a shirt or two, all the glass had hit the floor in front of Dave, trapping him in his chair.

She pointed at him. "He's what happened. He won't keep his hands to himself."

Rocco looked at Dave and then at her and doubled over with laughter.

"Sorry, doll, but I know him and knocked up ain't his thing." He looked down at the mess on the floor. "I'll take it out of tonight's tips."

She could barely afford the bus fare back home much less afford to pay for six pints of beer, glasses and all. "No." The word felt odd on her lips. "This is his fault. He's constantly touching me."

Rocco looked at her like she'd grown a hairy tooth from her chin. "He means no harm."

Eden rarely cussed but something inside her heated up. She pressed her hands to her stomach as if she were covering her baby's ears.

"Dammit, Rocco!" The bar got quiet and all eyes turned toward her. "The only thing he's missing is the stirrups. The man practically gives me a pap smear each time I pass him."

Dave lifted his hands in the air. "Dude, she's crazy. I never touched her."

Rocco looked between his friend and Eden. She knew what was coming before the words ever came out.

She was halfway to untying her apron when he said, "I can't have you accusing the customers of misconduct. You're fired."

She pulled a handful of Good & Plenty from her pocket and shoved them into her mouth. It would be the only good thing about her day.

CHAPTER TWO

THOMAS

Thomas Cross stood back and looked at his kitchen. It was a damn work of art. Thankfully Doc Parker had waived his realtor fees. The extra money gave him the funds to retile and upgrade the appliances.

Hard to believe now that he'd dragged his feet on the purchase of the property just because it was on Pansy Lane. No way did the name of a street reflect the masculinity of the man living there. That was evident by the slate gray tile on the floors and black granite countertops that screamed understated but manly.

While he hated to admit it, the Coopers were right. Quality was in the details. The brothers had developed a house that was environmentally friendly and easy to build. In the time it took Thomas to tile his floor, the brothers from Frazier Falls had nearly completed the build of Luke's house.

He slid his hand across the smooth stone surface of the counter. Quality was in the details, but so was integrity. Each time he thought about that word his blood boiled.

A tap at his front door saved him from going down memory lane. His boots thunked across the slate tiles of the kitchen to the wooden floors of his living room. It was boys' night out and the first of them had arrived.

He opened the door to Luke, who carried a six-pack and a take-and-bake pizza from Dalton's culinary school. If not for his ready-made meals, Thomas was certain half the town would starve. Cannon certainly would because his wife Sage couldn't even microwave with skill.

"Welcome. You can put that in the kitchen." He pointed over his shoulder past the living room decorated with black leather sofas and a big-screen television hung from the wall that could rival a theater.

Generally, all the guys gathered at the Brew-house, but the girls were there having a bridal shower for Marina, who was weeks away from popping. That only reminded him that he needed to get into her shop for a haircut before the baby was born. No telling how long she'd shutter the doors of Cove Cuts after the birth of her and Aiden's son.

Another rap at the door had him turning around to answer it again. This time it was Bowie and Cannon standing on the porch. Bowie held a tray of baked goods, no doubt made that day by his wife Katie. Cannon stood with his hands empty. It was always better for everyone if Cannon just brought himself.

As he went to close the door, a boot stuck inside stopped the progress. The big buckled leather monstrosity belonged to Dalton. The man always looked like he'd just climbed off his Harley or escaped from prison, but he was one of those gentle giants.

"I've got wings and stuffed tater skins. Is the game on already?"

Thomas checked his watch. It was pre-season football, so the games didn't count, but it was a game nonetheless and real men watched football.

"Should start soon." He picked up the remote from the coffee table and pressed the power to light up eighty-four inches of awesomeness.

"Damn, man, yours is huge." Cannon stood directly in front of the big screen.

Thomas laughed. "So I've been told."

"Your television, asshole."

"Oh ... right." Thomas knew exactly what he meant but couldn't pass up an opportunity to bust his balls. Cannon Bishop was just one of the many in town who'd succumbed to marriage.

"Where's Aiden?" Dalton asked as he flopped onto the sofa, his weight pushing it back at least a foot.

"He's watching Kellyn tonight, but Mark should be here soon. Poppy gave him a kitchen pass," Bowie said.

"You guys." Thomas shook his head. "You feel lighter now that your balls are in your wives' pockets?"

It was Luke who chimed in. "I'm not married, but I wouldn't turn her down if she asked me." He looked toward the oven. "Care if I fire it up?"

The door creaked open with Mark Bancroft peeking his head inside. "Is this where the party is?" He waved a bag of chips in front of him.

"Come on in. There's beer in the kitchen."

"Hope you don't mind, but I invited Tilden to join us. He looked a bit lost when the girls kicked him out of the bar."

Everyone turned to stare at him, but it was Dalton who spoke first. "What's his story? He seemed to just show up a couple years ago and disappear into the woods with Ray Bradley and Zachariah Tucker. Is the old man a relative?"

Mark shrugged. "Not sure what his story is, but he's a nice guy, if a bit quiet. He's unassuming."

Cannon chuckled. "Always better to remain on the down low if you're a bootlegger."

"That's the thing. He's not really a bootlegger. I'm sure he can make a good batch of shine if he wanted to, given he's around the stuff all the time, but he only helps old man Tucker with the wood deliveries."

"No shit," Thomas blurted. "You never know what you're going to get in this town. No one is ever what they seem." He picked up a beer and twisted off the cap.

"How so?" Luke asked.

Thomas gave him a do-you-have-to-ask look. "Look at Riley. She's granola and grain and born thirty years too late for Woodstock. You thought she was dangerous, and it turned out it was Meg we should have been watching all along."

Luke whistled. "That one there was trouble from the minute she rolled into town."

"Right?" Thomas took a long drink and continued. "And you"—he nodded toward Bowie—"you fall in love with a poor baker who turns out to have more money than God." He didn't stop.

"Dalton over here thought his little honey was an arsonist when in truth she was America's pop goddess."

"And me?" Mark asked.

Thomas laughed. "You're about the only one who knew what they were getting. But you don't count because you knew her all her life."

Thomas turned to Cannon. "You." He laughed. "You've got a woman who could mend you, kill you and comfort you, but I'll be damned if she can feed you."

The door opened and Wes Covington walked in. "Am I late?"

"Only for the relationship roasting." Luke turned to Thomas. "You got anything to say about Lydia?"

He shook his head. "Nope. She has to do my physical soon. Lydia is a saint." He smiled and plopped onto the other end of the couch.

Dalton opened his tray of wings and the guys moved in like vultures over roadkill. Luke pulled the pizza from the oven and it was half gone before the game began.

"Hey, man." Wes sat on the corner of the sofa, the only place besides the floor that was left. "Who was she?"

"Who?" Thomas knew exactly who Wes asked about. He wanted to know who had pissed

in his Wheaties and turned romance rancid
for him.

"Who broke your heart?"

Thomas laughed. "That's assuming I have a
heart." He tipped back the beer and turned the
volume of the television up.

While his friends focused on who would win
the pregame, Thomas resigned himself to having
lost the long game.

Sarah Blankenship had burned a hole so deep
inside his chest that there was no hope of recover-
ing. He didn't take her misdeeds out on other
women. He simply didn't engage. Sure, there was
a roll in the sheets from time to time. He was a
fireman and therefore needed to use his hose, but
he never stayed. He was too afraid of the backdraft
that a hot woman could cause. Once burned twice
shy, they said.

The first touchdown split the room in two.
They divided like oil and water with Bronco
fans on one couch and Steelers fans on the
other.

Thomas couldn't care less, so he took a seat on
the floor right next to the bag of chips and
watched his friends argue.

Just as halftime came so did a knock on the
door. He dragged himself to his feet and
answered.

Tilden stood on his porch, hands in his pockets, shuffling back and forth.

"I was told I could hang out with the guys."

His voice was deep, like Darth Vader deep, which was a surprise. While Thomas had never heard him speak, hearing James Earl Jones' voice come out of the maybe six-foot-tall man was a shock.

"Come on in." Thomas moved to the side to let him pass. "I'm Thomas." He pointed to the guys in the room. "You probably know the rest."

"I've seen you all around."

"There are beers in the kitchen, but I'm afraid the vultures have pretty much picked the bones of the meal clean. I think there's some leftover chicken in the fridge though."

He didn't consider himself a culinary wizard like Dalton, but Thomas could put together a decent meal. It was probably why he was the one that always cooked for the crew at the station.

"Nah, I'm good. I had the blue plate special at Maisey's."

"Right on." Thomas loved Maisey's specials too, and Thursday night was meatloaf and mashed potato night.

Tilden popped the top off a beer and came into the living room. He took a seat on the floor and seemed to blend into the woodwork.

After the next touchdown, which put the Broncos twenty-eight points up, the guys got restless.

"Do we get a tour?" Bowie asked.

Thomas stood and showed them around.

His master bedroom was a work in progress. It had the same deep tones that blended in with the rest of the house. Was it dark because of his mood or mostly black and gray because a guy couldn't go wrong staying monochromatic?

"I've got a second bathroom here." He pointed to the door off his bedroom. "I just installed a new tub and shower."

"Damn," Wes said. "Maybe you should work for me. That's good work in there." Wes was the resident builder. His family went way back in the town's history. There seemed to be a hierarchy of founding families. To Thomas' best recollection, there were the Parkers, the Bennett's, and the Bishops. Records he pulled up on his computer about the town's history also mentioned the Coolidges and the Carvers but there was some kind of land dispute between them and the Coolidges seemed to disappear sometime in the early 1880s.

He led them down the hallway to the first empty room on his right. "This will be my office when I have time to patch the holes and paint it."

The house had been vacant for far too long before he'd bought it. Turned out some of the kids from the next town over were into remodeling as well, and several of the walls were sporting foot-sized holes.

"Who owned this property?" Bowie asked.

Thomas shrugged. "Some investor who came in and bought up all the vacant homes as soon as word got out the Guild Creative Center was going up. His name is Mauri or Melton or something like that."

"Mason," Wes said with less enthusiasm than a cow at the slaughterhouse.

"You know him?" He moved through the Jack and Jill bathroom into the next room.

"Yep, he's the son of my father's best friend. Raleigh Van der Veen."

The quiet Tilden added, "Veen is Dutch for swamp."

Mark laughed. "So now you're a translator. Aren't you a surprise?"

Tilden melted back into the wall and took up his place at the end of the line.

"This, my friends, will be the man-cave within the next few days. Furniture is coming this week." He pointed to the long narrow room that was perfect for a pool table or ping pong. Hell, he could probably put a one-lane bowling alley in there if he wanted.

"What do you need with a man-cave?" Cannon asked. "The whole place is a cavern."

"You're just jealous." He leaned against the wall. "Try to put a he-room in the bed and breakfast and see how that goes."

"True." Cannon walked the length of the room. "The space is great, but it won't warm your bed, microwave your lasagna, or rub your back when it hurts."

Deep inside, Thomas knew he was trying to compensate for what would no doubt be more of a loss than a gain. He'd wanted all of the things these men had. In fact, he'd once had what they had and somehow his life had gone up in flames.

Thomas pushed the thought away. "You're right," he said. "But it won't bitch when I leave the toilet seat up. Won't care if I stick my clothes in the hamper, and it won't tell me what time to come to bed."

CHAPTER THREE

EDEN

The phone roused Eden from a deep sleep. Her voice broke the silence with a croak.

"Hello." She rubbed the sleep from her eyes and pushed Porkchop from the bed. She'd taken a liking to curling up between the rise of Eden's stomach and her chin.

"Hey, it's me."

Relief washed over her as her sister's voice filled her ears.

"Oh, thank God. How was the babymoon? I was certain you'd decided to stay in Bora Bora."

The silence on the end of the line was odd because generally, Suzanne ran her mouth like a broken faucet.

"Can you meet me in Breckenridge? I've got a

meeting there tomorrow afternoon, but I thought we could talk over breakfast."

"I'm not really supposed to drive long distances. It's—"

"You're pregnant, Eden. To most women that's not a handicap. It's a few hours in the car. Besides, the trees are turning colors, and you always loved that."

She considered her request. Because of how far her stomach stuck out, to remain comfortable, she had to push her seat way back and had a hard time touching the pedals.

"It's really uncomfortable, Suze, but yes, I can do it." There it was again, the inevitable yes that would eventually come about. It was better to acquiesce quickly than drag it on. Suzanne always got her way.

She hadn't become the vice president of the Alpine Hotel Chain because she was a poor negotiator. Sometimes Eden wondered if she rose in rank because everyone was afraid to say no to her sister. "Perfect. We really need to talk about the best way forward." She cleared her throat. "I've got a check for you."

That alone was worth the trip.

"Okay. Sounds great. You didn't answer my question about your time away with Brady."

"Got to go. I'll see you tomorrow."

Eden was left with so many questions but only silence remained. A moment later her phone dinged with a message from Suzanne's assistant telling her the place and the time to meet.

AT PRECISELY NINE in the morning, Eden walked inside the Hungry Bear Café in Breckenridge, Colorado. A quick glance around told her Suzanne hadn't arrived yet. It was no surprise. Her sister was a busy woman. She basically ran the resort chain, which had properties all over the world.

Eden was excited to hear about the newest acquisition in Bora Bora. She could only dream of staying in a bungalow on the water with a full staff that included a cook, a butler, and a housekeeper.

After sitting in the car for hours with the steering wheel digging into her stomach, she opted for a table.

Her hand rubbed lovingly over her belly. "Hey, little person, it's almost time to come out and meet your mommy."

Eden hoped that the birth would change her sister's life for the better. She stared toward the window thinking about a diner similar to this where her sister had told her she was infertile.

Thinking about it now make her throat swell with emotion.

Watching Brady and Suzanne cry over the fact that they'd never have a child was heartbreaking. How could Eden say no when they asked her to be a surrogate?

"You're going to have a rich, full life, little one, and I'll be the best aunt ever."

It took some time to get used to the idea of having her sister's child. Everyone, including Eden's mother, told her it was a bad plan. Their arguments were sound. Eden had never had a child of her own and giving up her first child would be impossible, but Eden considered it an honor to give her sister something that no one else could.

At twelve years apart, Suzanne and Eden never had much in common. Suzanne was off to college by the time Eden was six. All she'd ever wanted was to bond with her big sister and this was it. Or so she thought. It certainly had gone differently than the dream she'd put together in her mind.

In the fantasy, Eden and Suzanne would go to all of her doctor's appointments. Sadly, with her sister's busy schedule and the geographic difference of their lives with Eden living in Denver and Suzanne living outside of Breckenridge, they were together for the first appointment where the heart-beat was heard and the first ultrasound where the baby actually looked like a baby. She hadn't wanted to see "it" when it was a blob.

"Can I get you something to drink?"

Eden's head snapped up to the waitress who'd arrived while she was daydreaming.

"I'd love a glass of apple juice if you have it."

"Coming right up." The woman, whose nametag said Vi, looked down at her belly. "Someone else joining you?"

"Yes, my sister. She's late but should be here soon."

Vi spun on her sneakers and disappeared.

She glanced around the restaurant, not lacking in carved wooden bears and honey pots.

"You'll learn to ski and have grand vacations. You'll be able to go to college wherever you want. Your mom and dad are smart and successful."

That last comment made her laugh. No one really knew who the mom and dad were. Because at forty, Suzanne's eggs weren't viable, and they used a donor egg. Eden had offered up one of hers, but her sister said it would be weird for her husband's sperm to mix with Eden's eggs. Her exact words were, "It would feel like a part of him was cheating on me."

Vi swung by and dropped off the apple juice

before she headed for the new couple that had come in.

In the end, it was decided that donor sperm and a donor egg would be used. Her sister didn't want Brady to have more invested in their child than she did. So there was no DNA connection to any of them. Everything about this baby was a beautiful mystery.

All Eden knew was the father was tall and smart, with brown hair and blue eyes. The mother was blonde and petite like Eden and Suzanne.

The door opened and in blew her sister like a tropical force wind.

"Sorry I'm late." Suzanne's blonde tufts of hair reached for the sky. She looked around the diner. "I hate tables." She nodded toward the booth in front of the window. "Let's move."

Eden touched her stomach. "I barely fit in a booth."

Her sister rolled her eyes. "But you do fit, so let's move."

She wanted to say something, but often it was easier not to argue.

Suzanne was already tucked into the booth before Eden could roll to her feet. When she took her seat across from her big sister, she noticed the dark circles under her eyes.

"You okay?"

Her sister's upper lip quivered until she drew it between her teeth and bit down. It slipped out with a pop.

"Yep, I'm good." She lifted the menu up to her face. "They have French toast."

Eden's heart picked up. Something was wrong. Really wrong. Suzanne never touched carbs. The last time she'd put one in her mouth was when Brady asked her to marry him. While she was ecstatic at what she called the merger, the marriage meant she'd have to move away from Texas. It was how they ended up in Colorado. Brady and Suzanne for their jobs and Eden because she wanted to support her sister.

She reached over and lowered the menu to find streams of tears running down Suzanne's face. She leaned farther forward to swipe at them, but the table got in the way.

A thump of the baby's foot sent her back into the booth. "Your baby doesn't like the booth either."

Suzanne gave Eden's stomach a cursory glance before she waved Vi over and ordered French toast and a bagel with cream cheese.

She opened her purse and pulled out a check. "This should cover the hospital bills and this month's past due rent. I'm sorry about being late."

"Me too. The only reason I'm not homeless is

because I pulled double shifts the last two week-ends." She didn't want to tell her sister she was jobless, so she held that information back. "You want to talk about what's going on?"

Suze's lower lip found its way between her teeth. She chewed and gnawed until Eden was positive there'd be a hole left behind when she finally let it loose.

"The resort is great. Polynesia is perfect. The people are beautiful and accommodating." She took a deep breath. "So much so that I found Brady in bed with the maid." She pulled her fingers through her short, spiky hair. "Oh, who am I kidding? Brady has been with lots of maids, and secretaries and cocktail waitresses."

Eden's mouth dropped open. "For how long?"

Suze lifted her shoulders. "Since the beginning, I suppose." She let out a laugh that could make a serial killer cringe. "You don't think I made it to vice president because of my brains, do you?"

"Yes." Eden had always thought her sister was capable of anything she put her mind to. Never once had she considered that her quick rise in the corporation was because she'd been sleeping with Brady, who happened to be a leading shareholder in the company.

Suzanne shook her head. "That's your problem. You're too naïve. You take things at face value. You assume the best about people. You shouldn't."

Eden had so many questions. "If he's been unfaithful for all these years, why would you want to have a baby with him?"

Her chest expanded as she took in a breath. Her lips pursed when she let go of the air. "We thought it would be the fix to what was wrong in our marriage."

What could Eden say? She was twenty-eight, but she was far from stupid. Even she knew a baby wouldn't fix a bad marriage. "Now what?"

"He filed for divorce yesterday morning."

It was Eden's turn to suck in some air. She did it over and over again until she was dizzy. She gripped the edge of the chipped Formica table and tried to calm her runaway heartbeat. She was certain the baby did a flip inside her as her hands moved across to try and soothe.

"Okay." She let out little puffs of air. "You can do this. Lots of women have become single parents. It happens all the time."

Suzanne's eyes grew as round as Petri dishes. "No, you don't understand. I'm here to tell you that I don't want the baby."

Her mouth opened and shut several times, but nothing came out. Every cell in her body was screaming silently. Their mother was right. She said Suzanne would never be able to fully appreciate the gift of a child. She'd warned Eden several times to reconsider, but she'd been caught up in giving her sister the one thing she couldn't give herself. Even when she seemed less than enthusiastic about updates and not interested in decorating a nursery, Eden accepted it as Suzanne's way. She'd always had everyone else do everything for her. She delegated and things got done.

Had Eden just been another box to check off? Get a degree—check. Get a high-powered job—check. Seduce the largest shareholder—check. Climb the corporate ladder—check. Have an heir —check.

A rage unlike any Eden had ever felt boiled from deep inside her. The heat of her anger flamed her cheeks.

"You don't get to return your baby like an unwanted pair of shoes."

Maybe it was because Eden was usually so obliging and quiet, but her top of the lungs screaming blanched Suzanne's skin.

She leaned in toward the center of the table. "Keep it down. I don't want everyone knowing our business."

That really pushed Eden over the edge. "Oh my God, this is so typical. Your ego has no bounds. All my life I wanted to be like you. You were so pretty, so successful, so confident. You know what? You're such an asshole." She tried to move from the booth but in her anger, she managed to get herself wedged in the corner.

Suzanne pulled two twenties from her purse and slapped them on the table as she slid from the booth. "I can't deal with this right now. I've got a meeting." She looked at the check she'd placed on the table earlier. "That should take care of your expenses until the baby is born. Put it up for adoption and go on with your life."

"Are you kidding me? I'm weeks from having your child."

Her sister lowered her eyes. "I'm sorry. I really am, but we both know that's not my child. It's just a cocktail we mixed up." She swung her purse over her shoulder and walked out the door.

Vi moved forward with several plates in her hands. She set down the French toast, the bagel and cream cheese, and the eggs and bacon Eden had ordered. "Anything else?"

Eden broke into tears.

Vi gave her a pat on the shoulder. "It's just hormones. You'll see. Once that baby is born, everything will be all right."

Eden knew that nothing would be all right ever again.

CHAPTER FOUR

THOMAS

Was it possible to fall in love with a television? Thomas had thought eighty-four inches was huge, but the screen in his man-cave filled an entire wall. He moved the cleaning cloth across the surface as gently as he'd caress a woman's breast.

He stepped back and lowered himself into the soft leather of the theater seats he'd installed. They were like the hug of a thick-thighed woman. His favorite kind. He liked his women with a little meat on them. His favorite moments with Sarah were when she was at the last month of her pregnancy and everything was filled out and round and perfect. Loving on her lush body was like climbing inside of heaven. He'd lived in bliss until the day her water broke, and his world fell apart.

With the remote in his hand, he flicked through the channels until he found a ball game. Nothing cleared a man's mind of a woman like pigskin and sweat.

Fifteen minutes later he dialed his buddy Luke.

"Hey man, the beers are cold, and I've got hundreds of stations to choose from. Come on over."

"Wish I could, but Riley and I are heading into Copper Creek to pick out new furniture for the house."

"That's right. I forgot you were being domesticated."

"Call the others. I'm sure one of them will come to your rescue."

Thomas laughed. "I'm not the one that needs rescuing." His words were strong, but his conviction wasn't. He was certain if he kept talking to himself, he'd be crazy inside of six months. It baffled him to consider how many cable options he had and yet he still oftentimes felt lonely. "Go with black furniture. It matches everything."

His hand rubbed along the butter-soft arm of the chair.

"Wait until some woman comes along and insists you bring a little color to your life."

"If she's talking red stilettos, I'm in."

33

They hung up and Thomas called Bowie. He led with the same line. "Hey man, the beers are cold, and I've got hundreds of stations to choose from."

"Sounds great, but Katie and I are taking Sahara to the Denver Zoo. She has an obsession with monkeys."

"She's like two, how can she be obsessed with anything beyond naps and her mother's teat?"

Bowie laughed. "Katie's teats are off limits, my friend, and obviously you've never been around a toddler. Last week she wouldn't eat anything but dino-bites and fries. We had them for breakfast, lunch, and dinner. This week it's monkeys. We indulge where we can."

"What happens when it's football players and cell phones?" Thomas kicked out the footrest of his recliner and popped the top on his beer.

"I've got a shotgun and the nearest convent on speed dial." In the background Katie asked if Bowie was almost ready.

"I don't envy you."

"Yeah, you do, but that's a conversation for another day. I've got to go. My girls are waiting."

Thomas hung up and surfed the channels until he found a war movie. He could watch *Saving Private Ryan* a million times and never tire of it, but today it didn't interest him.

He picked up his phone and dialed Cannon.

"What's up?" his friend answered.

"My big screen television. I've got length and width."

"Braggart." In the background was the sound of Otis. No doubt Cannon was on the back patio and Otis was chasing birds.

"You got some time to come over and catch a game or a movie?"

"Nope. Sage and I are heading into town with Trigg and Charlie and the twins. We're going to check out that big box store that just opened in Silver Springs."

"You mean Costco?"

"Yeah, that's the one."

"Dude, it's like Walmart on steroids. You can skip it and not really miss anything. It's just like the corner store but everything comes in quantities of a thousand or more. Who needs a thousand of anything?"

Cannon laughed. "Apparently the parents of twin boys. They go through over a dozen diapers a day. Besides, the bed and breakfast is filled up solid for a few weeks and that means lots of hungry mouths to feed in the morning."

"If your wife cooked, you'd be set." Thomas thought about Sage and suppressed a laugh. It was a good thing she was a nurse.

"If my wife cooked, we'd all be dead." A muffled thump and a yelp sounded. "I'm just kidding, sweetheart. That mac and cheese you microwaved was delicious."

"Sounds like you need to go."

"Thanks for nothing, man. When Sage is mad, she doesn't withhold food. She withholds something far more satisfying than her cooking."

Thomas raised a hand to cover his ear. "I don't want the details." Once again, he hung up and was left on his own.

With the push of a button, his footrest went down, and Thomas rose from his chair. Maybe holing up inside all day wasn't the best idea.

The interior of his house was a masterpiece, but the outside was still a work in progress. On his porch he looked around. There were flowerbeds to clean out. A picket fence to mend. His grass needed a good mowing and trees needed to be pruned.

There were things in his budget he could afford to have done, but most were up to him. The hard work kept his mind on what he had and not what he didn't.

The afternoon was spent mowing, weed whacking, and nailing loose pickets.

"You're making me look lazy," called Mr. Larkin from across the street.

"You can always come over and lend a hand," Thomas shouted back. Mr. Larkin was at least eighty and no doubt nearly blind. One too many times in the short time Thomas had lived on the street did he inform the old man that he had on two different colored shoes or socks. It appeared he had ten pairs of the same shoes all in varying colors and condition. Maybe he was a fan of the big box store and bought things in bulk.

"You invite me over for a beer, and I'll consider it, but if all you want is free labor, I'm not your man."

Thomas tossed his hammer to the side. What the hell? "Come on over then. I've got a cold one for you now."

Mr. Larkin shuffled across the street without even looking. When he arrived, he was wearing shorts he had to have owned since the '80s and a pair of knee-high socks. One had a purple band of color and the other green.

"You like light beer or the darker stuff, Mr. Larkin?" Thomas led the man inside his home.

"Light beer is for pussies," the old man said. He squinted his eyes. "Call me Peter. Mr. Larkin makes me feel old."

Thomas wanted to tell him he *was* old but patted the man's back. "One stout coming up."

"This house used to belong to Mabel Kirkenheifer." Peter laughed. "When we were kids, we shortened her name to heifer."

Thomas poured the beer into a mug and handed it to Peter. "That wasn't nice."

He waved a hand through the air. "It was all in fun. She never took offense because she was tall like a basketball player with the shape of a string bean. No hips, no bottom and..." He moved his hand in front of his chest and tapped on his sternum. "No boobs."

He hated to ask but was curious as to the history of his house. He knew it was built in the forties just as the paper mill was being constructed. "What happened to her?"

"She died."

"Right." Thomas pointed to the living room. "You want a tour of the place?"

"Nope, I just wanted a free beer." He tipped back the mug and drank deeply. A mustache of foam was left behind when he lowered the drink.

"Her daughter inherited. That would be Abby Garrett. Not a damn thing like her mother. That girl is all sweet and honey."

Thomas wanted to groan. Abby Garrett had been after him since he'd arrived in Aspen. She was sweetness and honey, but she was also bees and hives. One thing Thomas wasn't a fan of was bees. She was also looking for forever, which didn't exist in his vocabulary. He'd finally had to sit her down one day and be honest. He hoped she'd move her sights to someone else soon, because despite his honesty, she stared at him like he was a flower and she was the bee.

"I thought she lived in the mountains?" He knew she had a bunch of land in the hills up Range Road. There was a clearing just over the ridge that opened up to acres of open land filled with wildflowers.

"She does. Her mother inherited that land from her grandfather who was a Carver, but Mabel liked the city."

Thomas laughed. "Aspen Cove is far from city living."

"Tell that to the girl who lives among a field of flowers." Peter moved into the living room and plopped onto the end of one of the sofas.

"I suppose it's all perspective. So, she sold the house and moved into the foothills?"

He shook his head. "She's got a sister and they split the property and assets. All Abby wanted was her bees and flowers. Her sister wanted warm weather and the beach. She packed up and moved to California."

He had been up to put out a small grass fire near Abby's place a few months ago. "Who owns the land next to hers?"

"That would be Bea Bennett. I've been waiting for someone to show up and claim ownership, but Bea's been in the ground for years now and no one's come a calling."

"There's always a mystery."

"What about you? You came in from Silver Springs I heard. You got no wife. No kids." He squinted and looked around. "No animals. What's your story?"

Thomas kicked off the wall he'd been leaning on. He moved to the vacant couch and took a seat. "Oldest story in the book. Met a woman, fell in love, didn't turn out well for me."

"Damn, son, one woman is not the end of the line when there's so many out there to choose from." He yanked up his falling sock and leaned forward. "I've been married twice. Bless both of their souls. Good women. One was an amazing cook and the other... well, let's just say she had other skills, but my life was richer for having both of them."

"Look at us now, both single."

Peter let out a laugh that shook the windows. "I'm single, but I ain't lonely. I'm old, but I ain't dead. I spend every Tuesday at Buttercups. Every Thursday I'm at Edith's from Frazier Falls. Mondays belong to Maria. She lives on Posey Road. That woman is no string bean, but she can make a mean casserole. I rest on Saturdays because the ladies from the church social club are very social after services and Wednesday is liver and onion night at the diner and no woman can outshine Maisey's liver and onions. I try to keep Fridays fluid."

Thomas simply stared at Peter. Did the old man, who no doubt set his teeth in a glass of water on the side of his bed each night, get more action than him? How was it that the highlight of Thomas's day was a beer and a big screen television?

"You're kidding, right?"

The old man finished off his beer. "Son, there are two things I never kid about. One is hemorrhoids and the other is women. It's time you found yourself the latter because sitting on your ass at home alone will give you the former."

Peter Larkin rose from his seat and shuffled to the door. "See you next Saturday, young man. I'll take the same beer but in a frosted mug next time." He walked out the door, leaving Thomas staring after him.

CHAPTER FIVE

EDEN

With Porkchop under her arm, Eden took one last look at her apartment. Without a job and no prospect of one, she couldn't afford to stay any longer.

The telltale shuffle sounded behind her and she turned to find Mr. Schubert.

"What's this about you leaving?" He pushed out a white envelope toward her chest.

"Yes, I'm heading north." Eden forced a smile to her lips as she looked at the envelope with the torn-open top edge and the address crossed out and replaced with her name.

"Most birds head south for the winter. You're a strange one, but you'll be missed." He stared down at his gnarled fingers and pushed the envelope a bit farther forward. "Got you a little something."

She was touched by his kindness. While she'd never been anything but nice to him, her internal feelings often didn't match what she portrayed.

"Thank you so much." She couldn't imagine what the man had put together. He lived off of his social security check and whatever he could find in the dumpsters and sell at the flea market on the weekend.

Eden had boxed up what she couldn't sell and gave it to him, certain it was a gold mine to a man with nothing.

She shifted Porkchop in her arms and peeked inside the envelope to find at least fifty coupons for diapers, wipes, and formula. Tears sprung to her eyes.

"Oh Mr. Shubert, you have no idea how touched I am from your thoughtfulness." She leaned over and kissed his scruffy cheek. "I'll miss you." In that moment, she was certain of it. He was a constant in her life. A constant pain in the behind, but a constant, nonetheless.

Nothing from this point forward would give her the same continuity as him "rushing" out of his apartment to meet the elevator.

"You take care of that baby now."

Her free hand went to her belly. "Yes, I'll definitely do what's best for the baby."

She turned and walked away before she could cry.

"Ready for an adventure?" she asked the cat. "Not sure how you feel about Alaska. Not sure how I feel about it either."

Porkchop curled into a ball on the passenger seat and fell asleep.

Eden had hit the outskirts of Denver when her phone rang. Her heart played hopscotch in her chest. She prayed it was Suzanne calling to tell her it was all a big mistake, but the ring was wrong. This was her mother's tone.

"Hey, Mom."

"Oh honey, I just talked to your aunt. She said there's a big storm moving through in a few days. If you don't get there before it hits you might have to wait several weeks."

"What? I can't wait several weeks. Mom, in several weeks I'll be at my due date. I'm already pushing it driving at eight months along."

The typical *tsk tsk* sound pushed through the phone. "I told you having your sister's child was a big mistake. Didn't I?"

"You did, but I just thought—"

"No, you didn't, and that's the problem. You assumed it was time for her to have a child. Decided it would be good for her. Felt sorry she couldn't have one herself. You know Suzanne; she wants everything she can't have. Don't you remember that call we got from the animal rescue center asking where to deliver the gazelle?"

"No."

"Well, you were probably too young, but your sister called and told them we'd be happy to place the animal on our acreage."

Eden thought back to their apartment in San Antonio. "We didn't have acreage. We had a back patio."

"Exactly my point."

"You're right." There was no point in arguing. Her mother hadn't been there the day Suzanne broke down and cried in her arms for over an hour, telling her how she'd had this grand plan to do things right. To marry, succeed in her career and have a child she could give the world to. It all seemed so logical and so heartbreaking that she'd get everything she wanted but the child.

"You're just lucky Aunt Cici has that big house in Fairbanks."

Lucky wasn't what she was feeling at this moment. Frustrated. Angry. Sad. Like she had to pee. Those were the things she felt.

"How are you, Mom?" After her father died ten years ago, her mother had met and married a

Department of Defense educator who took her to live in Japan. He taught ninth grade at the school at Misawa while her mom taught English to Japanese nationals.

"I'm doing okay, sweetheart. I'm sorry you're going through this but in a few weeks, you'll have the baby, put it up for adoption and you can move on with your life. Cici says there's a lot of bar work in Fairbanks and there's a lot of men."

"It's not my life's dream to be a cocktail waitress."

"No, but it is what you are."

Eden wanted to scream at the world at the unfairness of it all. Suzanne was over a decade older. College wasn't a maybe for her. Dad had paid for it. By the time Eden turned eighteen, her father had died and there wasn't a penny saved for her education. She took a few classes at the community college. Thought she'd study graphic arts, but then her mother met and married Stu. Everything else was history. Mom moved from Texas to Japan. Suzanne was en route to Denver for her job and Eden followed her there in an attempt to stay connected to family.

"I've got to go, Mom."

"Don't forget what I said about the storm."

"Yep, got it."

She hung up feeling lower than when she'd begun.

If an early storm was moving through Fairbanks, there wasn't much Eden could do. She was over 3000 miles from her aunt's place. Even if the conditions were perfect and she could drive fifteen hours a day, it would take her four days. Now that she was pregnant and had a bladder the size of a walnut, it would take her longer. She'd be lucky if she got there by next summer.

As she wound through I70 and headed north she'd finished off her last box of Good & Plenty. Things went from bad to worse. She'd stopped at two stores to get a fresh supply, but no one carried them. She had to settle for a bag of Mike and Ike's, which didn't quite quell the craving but would have to do.

As she moved through the mountain pass, she laughed and cried at her predicament. She was twenty-eight, single, pregnant with a mystery child, nearly broke except for the check her sister had given her, which would barely pay for the baby's delivery. She hadn't had time to contact any adoption agencies given that she'd basically had to move right away. She had less than a thousand dollars to make it to Alaska and all she wanted was a box of candy. How hard could that be? Add to that the constant pain in her lower back and she was miserable.

Having the steering wheel dig into her stomach made her certain her child was miserable too.

It struck her as funny to think about the baby as hers. She never had. She'd always known that the day he or she was born she would be an aunt, not a mother, but now it was different. This baby was just as much hers as it was anyone else's.

"Hey, peanut. How are you doing in there?" Guilt washed over her as she thought about the buckets of tears she'd cried over the last few days. Did he or she feel her sadness? There was no doubt this baby had a front row seat to her grief.

The pain in her lower back was almost unbearable. She was certain the cramped quarters were putting pressure on a nerve, so when the turnoff to Aspen Cove came about, she took a detour and hoped against hope that they would have a gas station and a box of pink and white black licorice candies.

She pulled into the station and took a deep breath. She gave Porkchop a between the ears scratch and told her to stay put.

That brought a smile to her face because Porkchop moved for no one and nothing but food. Eden opened the door and stepped outside. The briskness of the mountains was refreshing. The scent of pine hung in the air.

She rubbed at the pain in her lower spine and stretched, hoping to work out the kink that made her want to drop to her knees.

"When are you due?" A woman with a baby boy perched on her hip walked forward.

Eden looked around as if another pregnant woman were present. She pointed to her chest. "Me?"

The woman laughed. "You're the only one I see, although pregnancy seems to be a contagious illness here in Aspen Cove. I've caught it eight times. This is little Paul. He's the last of the Williamses to be born from me. I'm Louise." She stepped forward and pointed down Main Street. "The veterinarian just had twin boys. The sheriff's wife is due to have a baby in several weeks. She owns Cove Cuts."

"Oh, wow." Eden removed her gas cap and reached for the nozzle.

"Don't you touch that." Louise looked over her shoulder to the open bay garage. "Bobby, I need your help."

Eden heard a "Be right there, sweetheart" before a handsome man wearing blue overalls appeared.

"What do you need?" He walked by Louise and Paul and gave each a kiss. It was obvious to

Eden this was a couple in love and a thread of envy wound through her.

"She needs her gas pumped. No need exposing her or that baby to fumes."

"Got it." He walked toward Eden. "You need anything else?"

Just then her stomach growled. "I could use a snack."

"You come with me." Louise tucked her free arm through Eden's and led her into the garage, where a counter with a small selection of chips and jerky was on display. "What are you craving?"

Eden set her hands on her stomach. "It's always the same, Good & Plenty, but they're hard to find." She scanned the rack for candy but found none.

"I stopped ordering candy when Bobby gained the same amount of weight as I did when I was pregnant with this little guy. I think he was determined to go through all the aches and pains with me."

A laugh bubbled up from deep inside Eden. She'd had no one but herself. "That's okay." She looked over her shoulder. "Do you think the corner store would have them?"

"They might." She pulled a box from under the counter. "Shh. Don't rat me out, but Katie, our resident baker, made brownies today and put extra chips and nuts in them for me. I'll share with you, but if Bobby found out, they'd be gone in two bites. These were my go-to when I was pregnant. I couldn't eat enough chocolate."

Eden pulled out the smallest brownie and took a bite. It was a piece of gooey heaven. It would satisfy the sweet craving for a few moments at least.

Bobby walked in just as Louise tucked the box under the counter.

"I checked your oil, filled the tank, and checked the air pressure in your tires. You should be good to go." He looked at Louise and smiled. "It's $21.60." He reached over and wiped a speck of brownie from his wife's lip then sucked it off his thumb. "Hope she shared with you." He walked outside.

Eden and Louise looked at each other and broke into laughter.

"Damn man's too smart."

"You guys are great." Eden longed to be in a place that was carefree and kind.

"When are you due?"

Eden put the exact change on the counter. "I've got several weeks left."

"Where are you off to?"

"Alaska." Eden's voice cracked. "I'm visiting my aunt."

Louise shook her head. "That's going to be a long road trip. You could have planned a little better."

With a nod, Eden turned to leave. "You're right, but it's what it is for now. It was a pleasure meeting you, Louise." She turned around and came back to cup the baby's cheek. "You take care of your mom, she's a rare find."

Eden climbed back into her car and found a parking spot half a block down the road. Small shops lined the street. It was a town most likely built during the early to mid-eighteen hundreds. A time when all a town needed was a bar, a place to eat, and a whore house. She saw the bar immediately. Bishop's Brewhouse looked like the perfect place to go after a day of panning for gold or hunting bear. She scanned the other businesses. There was Bishop's Bait and Tackle, B's Bakery where Katie the brownie wizard must work, Maisey's Diner, a sheriff's office, Cove Cuts, a veterinary clinic, a medical clinic and pharmacy, and the Corner Store. Everything seemed to be open and running except a place called The Dry Goods Store.

Eden walked toward the corner and peeked in the windows on her way. It appeared that the Dry Goods place had been used as something recently, but maybe it was seasonal. With fall then winter approaching, she couldn't imagine a town as small as Aspen Cove would get much winter traffic.

Pushing through the glass door of the little convenience store, she was greeted with a warm hello.

"Welcome," a sweet older woman with salt and pepper hair said. She pushed against the older, overweight man snoozing behind the counter. "Phillip, wake up and say hello to our guest."

The balding man opened his eyes one at a time. "Dammit, Marge, she don't care if I say hello or not." He looked at Eden and smiled. "Afternoon. Can I help you find something?"

Eden wanted to laugh. If Phillip had been a cat, she would have called him Porkchop. He had the same rotund figure and laid-back personality.

"Where's the candy aisle?"

The man chuckled. "I wouldn't so much call it an aisle as much as a section." He pointed to his left. "Go down three rows and you'll see what we've got. If we don't have what you're looking for, you can check out Doc's because his candy selection is vast since Sage started working in the clinic. That girl loves her peanut cups and chocolate, and those little fruit drops."

"Phillip, they're called Skittles, and we have them too."

"Thank you." Eden moved down the rows and caught sight of a man to her right. He was hard to miss. Tall with dark hair. Shoulders wide enough to bear the worries of the universe, and an ass that no doubt if she was able to touch it would be hard enough to crack walnuts.

He hadn't noticed her, which gave her more time to gawk. Since she'd become pregnant, she hadn't had any men in her life. The most action she'd gotten was that day Dave had tried to examine her in public and that wasn't pleasant.

She really missed men. Missed the way their arms felt around her. Missed the hardness of muscles under her fingertips. Missed the smell of cologne and sweat. Yes, she even missed the smell of sweat.

Moving on down the row, she found the aisle of sweets. It wasn't a candy aisle but an everything aisle that included cookies, cakes, donuts, pastries, and candy. Eden perused the offerings looking for the white, pink, and black box that always brought a smile to her face. Funny how she hated black licorice before the baby, and now couldn't get enough of the stuff. It wasn't just the black licorice that she wanted. She loved to peel the candy coating away with her teeth and suck on the soft center until it disappeared. Her entire mouth would turn black, but she didn't care. It was her one guilty pleasure.

After skimming the aisle several times, she came to the conclusion that Phillip and Marge had poor taste in candy. She picked up a bag of Skittles and reached for a box of chocolate covered donuts. Since Skittles contained real fruit juice, she justified her purchase of the donuts. It was crazy because she never felt like she needed to justify the other things she ate.

Being petite, she couldn't reach the top shelf, so she stepped onto the lower one and hoisted herself up. She'd almost reached the object of her desire when a hand stretched over hers and grabbed the box.

CHAPTER SIX

THOMAS

Thomas had run out of just about everything. He moved down each aisle at rapid speed tossing items in his handbasket like a contestant on a shopping show. When he turned down the sweet's aisle, he saw a petite blonde and stopped to look. Though he could only see her from behind, what he saw was nice—real nice. Rounded hips and jeans that hugged her thighs like a glove. He followed the dips and swells of her curves. Nice bottom and thick thighs that narrowed to slim knees and muscled calves. She wasn't from around here, but he hoped she was staying for a day or two.

It was when she turned around and he caught

sight of her swollen stomach that his gut twisted. A thousand thoughts went through his head. The first was where was her man?

He looked around the store and found no one but her, Marge, and Phillip. A woman in her condition shouldn't be traveling alone on the mountain roads where wildlife abound, and the weather was unpredictable. It was mid-September, but that didn't mean a few feet of snow couldn't fall overnight.

When she reached for the donuts and couldn't grab them, he started forward to offer help. When she stepped onto the bottom shelf he nearly ran in her direction.

His hand touched hers as he picked up the chocolate covered mini donuts. "You shouldn't be climbing on shelves in your condition."

"I'm height challenged." She looked down. "Kind of look like a Weeble these days. I figured I may wobble, but I won't fall down."

She smiled and his heart nearly melted, but one look at her stomach pulled him back to reality. Actually, took him back years before when he was preparing to be a father. When he and Sarah spent every Saturday shopping for the week's groceries. He was big on protein and vegetables and she had a thing for raspberry Zingers, but he always talked her down from three boxes to one. He wasn't worried about her weight. He never cared too much about those things. You loved a woman for her heart, her integrity, and her spirit. A beautiful body was a bonus but not a necessity. In Thomas's mind, there was nothing more beautiful than a woman pregnant with his child.

He remembered how proud he'd been to show Sarah off. He could have stood in the middle of the store and pounded his chest and told everyone to look at what he made. What a damn fool.

"Thank you for your help." Her hand went behind her back to rub and she winced.

"You okay?"

She nodded and turned toward the aisle that led to the register. He moved through the rest of the rows tossing in things he'd need during the week. Staples like milk and eggs and bread and butter. He moved back to the sweets aisle and swiped the last box of chocolate donuts from the top shelf. Why not?

She was on her way out the door when he arrived at the register.

"Cute little thing, that one," Marge commented.

While Phillip rang up the groceries, she bagged. Her attention was split between *Wheel of*

Fortune playing on the television behind the counter and whatever was happening outside.

Marge gasped and dropped the carton of eggs to the floor.

Thomas turned to see the young woman grip her stomach and fall to her knees. Being a fireman, it was second nature for him to respond.

Out of the door in seconds, he moved toward her like a bullet train.

"I'm here." He laid her out on the concrete and took her pulse. The poor thing had the heartbeat of a hummingbird. "Tell me what happened." He checked her for injury but could see nothing obvious other than the fact she was very pregnant.

Her face twisted and her body tensed. "Dammit." She pushed short puffs of air from her mouth. "I think I'm going to have the baby."

Thomas looked around. A few tourists had gathered around them.

Katie had come out of the bakery to see what the commotion was.

"Oh my. Should we get her to Doc Parker's?" She wiped her flour-covered hands on her apron and asked the few people blocking the sidewalk to step aside. "Can you walk, or should I have Doc bring the gurney?"

"No gurney," she said breathlessly. "I'll wa—"

Thomas watched as her mouth pinched in pain. "I got you." He swept her into his arms, holding her closely to his chest and moved with her down the street toward the clinic.

The bell above the door rang and Agatha looked up. "I'll get Paul," she said and scurried up the stairs to their apartment above.

Thomas had been in the clinic plenty of times, so he knew his way to the exam room.

Katie was hot on his heels with her phone in her hand. "I texted Sage and Lydia. They'll both be here in a moment."

"Thank you." With a kick of his boot the exam room door opened, and he carried the woman inside. "What's your name, darlin'?" He gently placed her on the table and stood beside her. His fingers naturally brushed the strands of hair stuck to her cheek aside.

"Eden. I'm Eden."

"Well, Eden. We're in a bit of a pickle here. Looks like you might be having a baby. Should I call someone?"

"I can call," Katie called from the door holding up her phone.

A tear slipped from Eden's eye.

"No, there's no one to call."

Thomas couldn't believe that. She hadn't

gotten pregnant by herself. There was certainly someone to call.

Bitter bile rose to his throat. He'd never forget delivering his daughter and seeing her ten perfect fingers and ten perfect toes. How he'd cried when they handed him the scissors and he severed the physical tie she had to Sarah. Little did he know that five minutes later, his ties would be severed as well.

"There's got to be someone. Surely you have family."

She shook her head. "No, there's no one."

"What have we got here?" For an old man, Doc Parker moved with swift efficiency.

Thomas went into first responder mode. "I have a thirty-something female showing signs of labor. Her pulse is 120 and erratic. Her name is Eden."

"I'm twenty-eight," Eden responded.

"Her hearing is fine." Doc picked up his blood pressure cuff and stethoscope from the table and went straight to getting a reading. "148/100." Doc shook his head. "Not good. Do you have a history of high blood pressure?"

Eden's hands cradled her belly. She looked at Thomas and back to Doc.

"No, I've been healthy so far." She lifted to

her elbows. "The pain has stopped. I should be fine."

Thomas pressed on her shoulder until she lay prone on the table again. "Let Doc Parker examine you. What I saw outside needs to be explored."

He desperately wanted to touch her pregnant belly. Wanted to see if it contracted until it was tight as a drum or if she was experiencing Braxton Hicks contractions that seemed like the real deal but weren't.

Sage raced into the room with Lydia right behind. Both women were tying their hair back into ponytails.

Doc Parker gave Lydia a look that Thomas recognized. It was one that said he was concerned but wouldn't scare his patient.

"Why don't we get you changed into a gown?" Lydia said and placed a blue and white cotton gown on the edge of the exam table. "My sister Sage is an RN with years of experience in labor and delivery. She can help you." She held out her hand to Eden. "I'm Doctor Lydia Covington. I'd like to examine you and see how far along we are."

Eden made an attempt to sit and scrunched her eyes closed again. "Oh, my God, not fun."

"Not as fun as the getting there, I bet," Doc

said. He turned to Thomas. "Shall we leave them to get changed?"

"No, I'm staying." He moved behind Eden.

Doc Parker lifted his bushy brows skyward. "Son, unless you've got a major secret and that baby over there is yours, I'm pretty sure you'll be waiting in the hallway like all the other strangers."

Thomas wasn't sure what was up with him, but on one hand he had this crazy urge to protect Eden, and on the other, he wanted to run as fast and far away as he could.

"Sorry, I don't know what I was thinking."

"Thomas?" Eden reached for his hand. "Thank you so much for your help."

He cupped her cheek and smiled. "You're welcome, Eden. Good luck to you and your baby."

He stepped out of the exam room and took a seat on a chair in the hallway.

"Do you know the girl?" Doc asked.

He shook his head. "No sir. I just happened to be there when she collapsed to the ground."

Doc stared at him for a long hard minute. "Why don't you stick around for a bit? I may need your help after all."

Doc rose and walked to the door. Leaving Thomas to his thoughts and memories.

Sarah's daughter was turning five years old next week. It had taken two years to not think of her every day. Another year to stop hating his ex-girlfriend for her betrayal. He should have hated the man who showed up minutes after the birth claiming to be the father, but he couldn't because he'd want to know. Why was Eden keeping her child a secret? There was definitely a father who had a right to know his child would likely be born today.

CHAPTER SEVEN

EDEN

"How far along are you?" Sage asked as she helped Eden change from street clothes to a medical gown.

Her elastic paneled jeans fell to the floor and she looked down at her stomach as if seeing it for the first time. "I'm due in about 4 weeks." She gathered her clothes and folded them hastily.

As Eden moved back to the exam table, she took in the office around her. In Thomas's arms, she couldn't see much on her way inside but for the black cotton of his T-shirt where she'd buried her head. If she breathed deeply, she could still smell his cologne floating on the air. It was a mix of pine trees and amber. Very outdoorsy and clean, not like the city men who bathed in patchouli and citrus scents.

Now that he was gone and no longer distracting her senses, she looked at her surroundings. The small office was bright and fresh with the expected posters of the skeletal system, but one wall stood out. On it was a rainbow of letters that said, "Happiness is the only contagion we hope you pass on." Just looking at the message made Eden feel better. So far, she'd been treated better by strangers than she had by family.

Sage picked up Eden's clothes from the exam table and set them neatly on a nearby counter. "Okay, that's good." She grabbed a file from a cabinet and began asking Eden questions.

"Full name?"

"Eden Summer Webster."

"Primary physician?"

"I've been seeing Dr. Oden Clark."

Sage smiled. "I know him, he's an excellent doctor. Can we give him a call and tell him we have you here?"

Eden was back on the table before she knew it. The two women had ghosted around her like a well-oiled machine. The table was extended, and she was on her back ready for the exam.

"Yes, but—"

A knock sounded on the door and Sage said, "We're ready."

"How's our little mother doing?" Doc Parker walked inside and stood at the head of the exam table.

Lydia took the stool at the foot. She rolled it forward and moved the sheet to Eden's knees. "We were just going to take a look."

Sage moved away, and Doc took her place with the file and the questions. They really had the art of distraction down. There was so much going on around her that she wasn't sure who was doing what.

"How long have you been having pains?" Doc asked. He pulled a pen from his lab coat and began jotting down notes.

She turned her head to face him. "They just started out of the blue."

"What about back pains? Have you had any?"

Eden whooshed out a breath of air. "All morning, my lower back has been hurting but I figured it was because I was driving and the little guy here was pushing against a nerve."

"It's a boy?" Sage wheeled what looked like an ultrasound forward.

"Oh, I don't know for sure. It was supposed to be a secret." She smiled. "I just figure with the strength of the kicks I was going to have a punter or a soccer player."

"Maybe a female martial artist," Sage teased.

"This is going to be a bit of pressure," Lydia said with one hand on Eden's stomach. She proceeded to do an internal exam and shook her head.

"What? Is something wrong with the baby?"

Lydia smiled. "Nope, and I don't think you're in labor. Zero dilation. No softening. Everything is where it's supposed to be at this moment." She pulled the sheet over Eden's legs but exposed her stomach. "Is this where you're hurting?" Lydia moved her hand over the baby bump—now more like a baby mountain.

Eden sucked in a breath. "Mmm-hmm." The urge to practice labor breathing began again.

"Diastasis Recti?" Doc moved forward to watch Lydia's hand roam over Eden's tummy.

"Oh, my God, is that bad? What about the baby?" Her breaths became rapid and shallow.

Doc set his hand on her shoulder. It was the kind of comforting touch she needed. There was no stress or urgency, just a gentle squeeze that reminded her not to panic.

"You'll be fine, and so will the baby." He pulled on a pair of gloves. "How about we take a look at the little one so you can see your child is perfect and healthy."

Doc didn't give her much notice before he squeezed a glob of cold gel onto her stomach. He pressed a wand against the skin and the comforting *swoosh, swoosh, swoosh* of the heartbeat moved through the air like a love song.

All four of them stared at the screen.

"Do you know the sex or want to know?"

Sage turned off the monitor before Doc could move the wand and reveal. "Mrs. Webster wants it to be a surprise."

"Fair enough." Doc handed the wand to Sage and pulled up a chair beside the exam table. "Should we be contacting Mr. Webster?"

"No. There's no Mr. Webster."

Lydia and Sage moved around the room cleaning up while Doc talked. "When will you be seeing your physician again?"

Eden took in a shaky breath. "Never."

Something fell to the floor and all eyes turned to Sage.

"Sorry." She stepped forward so Eden didn't have to strain to see her. "Was there a problem with Dr. Clark's care?"

"Oh no. It's just..." Her eyes filled up with tears. "I've had some setbacks recently, and I'm forced to relocate. I packed up my car and—" Panic set in. Eden swung her legs over the table and sat straight up. "Porkchop. Oh, my God. I forgot about Porkchop."

Doc held up a hand. "Groceries can wait."

"No, it's my cat. She's in the car."

Doc rose from his seat and peeked out the door. "Thomas, Ms. Eden's cat is in the car. Can you take care of it?"

"Yes, sir. Is her car the silver SUV?"

Doc looked toward Eden, and she nodded. "There's a carrier in the back."

Doc closed the door. "Porkchop should be fine. Thomas is a good lad." He took his seat again. "Sage is going to help you get dressed, and then, you and I need to talk."

Ten minutes later, Eden was sitting on a chair in the corner of the room. Doc sat across from her.

"This is what I've got so far. Your circumstances have changed. There is no Mr. Webster or other family to count on. You're eight months pregnant and on the road to someplace else."

She nodded. "Alaska."

His head shook back and forth. "As your new doctor, I have to advise against that."

"Why?" Eden had a plan. It wasn't a great plan but one, nonetheless. She had four weeks to figure out her life. It would take one of those weeks to get to her aunt's house. Hopefully, in the following three, she'd be able to come up with the

70

rest. Her hands went straight to the movement of her belly. These were the times she loved the most. It was almost as if the baby was telling her it would be all right.

"You're in no position to drive to Alaska. I've got a mind to call Oden Clark and ask why he'd allow that to happen. Your blood pressure is the biggest concern. Sage is running a urine sample to check for protein. High blood pressure is a sign of pre-eclampsia, a dangerous condition during the late stages of pregnancy. While you and your child are safe right now, as your current physician, I'm not willing to bet my license that you'll stay that way."

"I'm in danger of losing the baby?" Her heart rose to her throat to nearly choke her. There was no way she'd endanger her child.

"Your blood pressure is dangerously high."

"What about the pains?"

"Not related. It looks like the strain on your abdominal muscles has reached its peak. There may be a muscle separation, which is not uncommon. I'd say you overextended and pulled or tore a muscle that will most likely heal on its own."

Her shoulders rolled forward. "Donuts."

"Excuse me?" Doc took off his glasses and rubbed the bridge of his nose.

"I stood on a shelf and reached for donuts.

That man that brought me in here got them
for me."

"That would be Thomas. He's a fireman in
town. He's going to look after Porkchop while
we're having a talk."

Eden covered her face with her hands. The
entire last few weeks swept over her in a wash of
emotion.

"There's not much to talk about. My life is
falling apart. I have one option and that's to get
into my car and race toward Fairbanks."

"Race?"

Her nose stuffed up and she took in a shud-
dering breath. "Big storm moving in. If I don't
leave now, I'm going to get stuck in the center
of it."

Doc nodded his head. His old wise eyes narrowed. "I heard about that. It's an early storm
that's supposed to lock down the roads for days.
You really should wait for it to pass. Don't you
have anyone you can call? Anyplace you can go?"

Pointing out how desperate Eden's situation
had become was the blade that sliced her emotions
clean through. The tears welled up and spilled
forth.

"No, I have no one." She rubbed her hands
against her belly. "I'm pregnant with someone
else's child. They decided at the eleventh hour

they no longer wanted a baby. I was supposed to be an aunt and now I have to give my niece or nephew up for adoption because Suzanne doesn't want it?" she wailed.

Doc looked at her like she was speaking in tongues.

"This isn't your child?"

She shook her head. "No. This is my sister's child." She thought about it for a moment. "Actually, no one shares any DNA with the baby. It was a donor egg and sperm." She went on to explain how her sister didn't want her husband to have a bigger claim to the baby, so they decided to not share either of their DNA.

"Eden, DNA doesn't make you a family. It just makes you related." He gave her a thoughtful look. "You've carried this baby all these months, what are your plans now?"

She fell into a new crying fit. "She told me to give it up for adoption."

Doc reached for the box of tissues on the counter and set them in her lap. "Is that what you want to do?"

Her hands protectively held on to her baby—her baby. "No, but I don't have any choice. I have no job. There's no one to help me or support me. I don't want to bring a baby into the world and not be able to care for it."

Doc leaned back in his chair. "Do you care for your baby?"

"Oh yes. I love my baby. I love him or her so much that I'd be willing to give them up if that's the best option."

He stood. "You've told me several times now that this is your baby, so let's figure out a plan. No one is taking this child that you've loved and cared for all this time away from you."

"But how?"

"You leave that up to me. Stay put." He walked out of the room and within a few seconds Sage and Lydia returned.

They pulled up chairs to sit beside her. Lydia took a bottle of water from the pocket of the lab coat and twisted off the cap. "You need to stay hydrated."

She drank deeply, fearing all the tears she'd shed had dried her out. "Did Doc tell you my problem?"

Both women shook their heads. "Nope, all he said is that you'd be staying in Aspen Cove for a bit, and he needed to make some arrangements," Sage said. "I own a bed and breakfast, but sadly it's booked solid for the next several weeks. All the die-hard outdoorsmen are getting in their final fishing days."

"You own a bed and breakfast and you work as a nurse?"

"And her husband owns the bar, so she spends quite a few hours pulling the taps too."

Eden wiped at her tear-stained face. "Wow, and I thought working at Rocco's was exhausting." The tears built again and ran silently down her cheeks.

"You don't need to worry. Doc will figure it all out. The people of Aspen Cove are kind and generous."

"But I'm a stranger."

Lydia laid her hand on Eden's shoulder. "There is no such thing here. You're either a friend or a friend we haven't met. We've met you, so now you're a friend. No one turns their back on a friend."

Eden let out a semi-hysterical laugh. "No, you have to be related for that kind of dismissal."

The sisters looked at each other. "Sounds like it's time for a change."

CHAPTER EIGHT

THOMAS

Thomas stared down at the cat cowering in the corner of the carrier. It was a good thing he'd had some experience with Mrs. Brown's cat Tom, and he might not have had the foresight to take his shirt off and wrap it around his arm before he reached for the beast. Porkchop his ass, that cat was Lucifer with a pink sparkly collar.

His shirt, now covered with fur, was more orange and white than black. He thought they called this breed a tabby cat, but this was a crabby cat.

The door to the exam room opened and out walked Doc. He sat down beside Thomas and lowered his eyes to the pet carrier on the chair beside him.

"So, this is Porkchop." Doc pressed his finger

through the grate of the cage, but Thomas yanked it back.

"You want to lose a limb?"

"That bad, huh?"

"Like a damn Gremlin, fed well after midnight."

"Can't be all that bad." Doc brushed his finger against the grate again and the cat rubbed its head into him like it was begging to be petted.

As soon as Porkchop began to purr, Thomas huffed, "Damn traitor."

"I'm sure it was scared, that's all." Doc grabbed Thomas's hand and pushed it toward the cage. As soon as he neared, the cat's back arched, and a growl as big as a lion came out.

"Cat hates me."

Doc chuckled. "He'll get used to you."

Thomas cocked his head. "He won't have to. How's Eden? Is she going to have a baby?"

Doc moved his veiny hand through his hair leaving the strands pointing to the sky. "Yes, eventually she will, but not today."

Thomas let out a breath he wasn't aware of holding. He didn't know the woman. He shouldn't care one bit about her, but he did because caring was in his nature.

"That's good. She can get back on the road to wherever she's headed."

77

That's when he knew there was more to the story. Doc was friendly but he rarely took a seat and chatted about cats. He was sitting next to Thomas for a reason, and by the look on his face it wasn't good.

"She was headed to Alaska."

Thomas's mouth fell open like a broken hinge. "Alaska? That's over a three-thousand-mile drive. She can't drive that far in her condition."

Doc leaned back and kicked out his feet. Thomas noticed the Crocs he wore. They weren't his usual attire. Doc was old fashioned. He showed up to work in a button-down shirt and trousers every day. His black shoes were spiffed up and shiny no matter the weather—but then again, it was Saturday, and this wasn't an open clinic day.

"Those are my sentiments exactly. Even if her health was topnotch, I wouldn't have consented as her doctor to let her drive across country but ..."

"And her doctor did? Maybe you should call him. She could turn around and go back to where she came from."

"Now listen here, son."

Thomas knew those were the words that should bring fear to his soul. He'd been warned by Cannon and Bowie, Trig and Dalton, Luke and Mark and Aiden. Those four words meant a lesson was coming and a life was likely to change.

"Oh no you don't. I'm not up for a lesson today. I've got stuff to do and people to see."

Doc raised his bushy brow. "Oh yeah, what people?"

Thomas pressed his mind for something that would make sense, but he didn't want to lie. "It's fried chicken night at the diner. I've got a date with two thousand calories of deep-fried sexiness."

"Maisey closes at eight. You've got time, and I need your help."

He looked at the feline who was now rolled into a circle in the back of the cage. "I'm not taking the cat."

A long, exaggerated breath left Doc's lungs and he seemed to shrink in his chair. "I'm asking for more than that, son."

He was laying it on heavy. Calling him son always got Thomas right smack dab in the center of his chest. He missed his father. Wished they lived closer, but his dad preferred sunshine to snow and gators to grizzly bears.

"Okay, I'll take the cat for the day, but that's it." He turned to the cage. "You better be nice, or I'm not giving you any treats." The cat perked up and moved toward the front of the cage with a meow.

"Seems like you found her language." Doc leaned forward and rolled to his feet. "I'll let Ms. Webster know that you'll be happy to take them in until her child is born."

The floor fell out from beneath Thomas's feet. "Wait. What?"

"Ms. Webster is in an awful predicament that makes returning home impossible and moving forward perilous. She's eight months pregnant, with high blood pressure and no options but you."

Thomas's head rocked like a pendulum. "Oh no. I can't have a pregnant woman in my house. I don't do pregnant, and I don't do women."

Doc smiled. "Is that right? I had no idea." He reached forward and patted Thomas on the back. "Makes no matter what your preference is. I know you'll do the right thing."

How did his sexuality end up in question? "Doc, I do women." He could feel the heat of embarrassment rise to his cheeks. "Geez, you know what I mean. I'm just ... just not comfortable around pregnant women."

Doc nodded. "They're harmless really unless they don't get something they crave. With my Phyllis it was French fries dipped in ice cream, but not just any ice cream. She had to have that fancy chocolate with chocolate chips ice cream from Häagen-Dazs. My Charlie was a pricey one

but worth it. Survival will come down to being observant. All you need is to figure out what her
thing is."

"Donuts."

Doc laughed. "See, you're already ahead of
the game." He turned toward the room. "I'll let her
know you'll take her home."

He rushed forward, almost knocking the cat
from the chair. The kennel shook and the cat let
out another primal big cat growl. Thomas turned
around and picked the box up. "Quiet or no
treats." He really had figured out the damn cat
and now he had to figure out the rest. "Doc, I've
got a history that makes it impossible to take in a
pregnant woman. Too many hurts and too many
wounds. Can't she go to the bed and breakfast?"

"Booked full."

"What about the apartment over the bakery?"

"You know that's rented by Riley's brother
Baxter. Besides, no stairs. Her abdominal muscles
are struggling to support the baby. The stairs will
not be a good idea."

Thomas considered all the homes in town.
Most were two stories. Those that weren't were
uninhabitable. There was the Williamses' home,
but their house was busting at the seams. He
wouldn't wish a night surrounded by eight children on anyone. Katie and Bowie's house had a

half flight of stairs so that was out. That was the case with Dalton and Samantha as well as the new house Luke was building on the shore.

"Doc, please don't ask me to do this."

Doc walked back to the chair and sat.

Thomas took the same place beside him.

"Son, I don't have any choice. Sometimes we have to do what's right for others even if it's not right for us." He set his hand on Thomas's shoulder in the same manner his father would have done. "I can't force you to take her in. She's a stranger. We don't know her."

Thomas laughed. "I didn't think you'd ever met a stranger."

"You know the saying ... a stranger is someone you haven't met yet."

Elbows on knees, face in hands, Thomas rubbed the scruff of his jaw. "Eden is no stranger. I met her. I carried her here. She's simply a friend in waiting." He rose slowly to his feet. "Should we let her know she won't be sleeping in her car?"

"I knew you were a good lad." Doc led the way into the exam room.

In the corner sitting on a chair sipping a bottle of water was Eden. The discomfort was gone from her face. In its place was a beautiful smile.

Sage and Lydia rose from the chairs beside

her. "We'll be heading out unless you need us," Lydia said.

"If you need anything, you know where to find us," Sage added.

They left Eden alone with him and Doc Parker.

Thomas leaned uncomfortably against the counter several feet away while Doc took a seat to Eden's right. She moved her head left to right as if looking for something.

"Porkchop is fine," Thomas reassured her. "She's in the hallway. Do you want me to get her?"

"Would you?"

He was gone less than a minute and returned with the mewling animal.

Eden opened the cage and nuzzled the cat, who seemed to talk to her as if she had a tale to tell.

"Is that right?" Eden giggled. "A man rescued you and brought you to me?" She looked up at Thomas with gratefulness in her eyes. "Well, he rescued me and brought me here."

Thomas chuckled. "I'm not sure those are her words." He glanced down at his fur covered T-shirt.

Eden made a move to stand but winced and held onto her lower stomach. "This is a lesson in why donuts are bad for your health." The cat jumped from her lap and moved around Thomas's leg.

He leaned over and picked the animal up. "In front of your mom you're going to be nice but the minute she turns her back you'll expose your razor-sharp claws." He shook his head. "Typical woman."

Eden's eyes grew wide. "You don't have a high opinion of women, do you?"

Doc looked back and forth as they spoke.

"I let each woman I meet show me who they are." He wasn't sure how much he should say. Whether he should say anything at all. He would do the right thing because he was raised that way and Doc had played on those emotions, but she needed to know what she was getting when she agreed to stay with him. He wasn't going to change just because of her. "And I'm rarely surprised."

"That must be a comfort. People shock the hell out of me all the time."

"Well, Eden. I brought Thomas in here because he has kindly offered to let you stay at his house until you deliver your child."

Her brown eyes narrowed until a crease furrowed her brow. "Oh no. I'm heading to Alaska."

"Now, Eden, we talked about this. It's not safe for you to travel."

"While it's not recommended, I'm not sure it's unsafe. I'll stop and move every two hours. I'll drink lots of water. I'll get at least eight hours of sleep a night."

"You're avoiding the truth. There's a major storm heading toward Fairbanks," Doc reminded her.

She seemed to wilt under the weight of his words.

"Okay." She glanced up and Thomas swore her lower lip quivered.

If there was one thing he couldn't handle, it was tears. He'd do anything to get a woman to stop crying. It took him two long strides to get to her, lower to his haunches and thumb up her chin. "Hey, it's okay. Let's box up that cat and I'll get you to your new digs."

She took in a shaky breath. "You look like you want a houseguest about as much as you want the chicken pox."

"Given the option, I'd take the pox. At least I'd know what I was in for, but here we are. You need a place, and I've got one."

Porkchop had wheedled her way into his lap and every swish of her tale was a furry slap to his face.

Doc rose and walked to the door. "Seems like you kids have this under control." He looked over his shoulder. "Eden, I want to see you every day for the next week to check your blood pressure." He pointed to the ceiling. "I live upstairs, and I'll hear the bell when you come in." He smiled and shook his head. "Not true. Lovey will hear the bell, and she'll come get me."

"Lovey?"

"My sweetheart, Agatha. Damn woman is crazy to love an old fart like me, but she does, and I'm not investing in therapy to cure her."

Eden let out a heartwarming laugh.

Thomas didn't want to like her, but he'd do just about anything to hear that sound again.

"You kids be good. And Thomas ... she probably likes fried chicken too."

CHAPTER NINE

EDEN

As soon as the nice old doctor was out of earshot, Eden turned to Thomas. She couldn't help but stare at his eyes. They were soulful eyes. Eyes that had seen a lifetime of emotion. Blue eyes the color of a stormy day ringed by moss green with specs of golden sunshine scattered throughout.

"I'm so sorry you got roped into something simply because you were kind enough to come to my rescue. Rest assured, I don't expect you to take me into your home."

He stood, and his body hovered above her like a giant oak tree shading her from the harsh overhead lighting.

"While this is not what either of us had

planned, I'm a man of my word, and I will offer you a place to stay."

Eden slowly pushed to her feet, cradling her belly for support. "No need." She looked to the door. "Once I get Porkchop in her cage, I'll get back on the road."

His hands came to rest on her shoulders. It wasn't the type of pressure that kept her in place but a touch of reassurance.

"Not a chance." He glanced toward the door. "That man is like a god in these parts. To disappoint him is like showing your parents a poor report card. I'm not about to earn an F in his eyes." He leaned down and scooped up the cat, putting her back in her carrier. "You think she'll be okay in your car while we grab a bite to eat or should we drop her off at the house?"

It never occurred to her to question anyone's kindness, but this man was a stranger. While he looked nice and was obviously respected by Doctor Parker, Eden didn't know him. For all she knew, he could be the Colorado equivalent of Ted Bundy.

"I don't know you, and I'm not in the habit of staying with strange men, so if it's all the same to you, I'll grab my cat and be on my way."

She could see by his frown that he was grappling with indecision.

88

"Tell you what. Let's have some of that fried chicken Doc mentioned. The diner is just down the street. We can get to know each other a bit more. Happy to print out my resume and references. At this point, your situation calls for something more than status quo." He picked up the carrier and headed for the door. "I'm not one to invite strange women to stay in my house either. It would appear we have that in common."

He stood at the door and waited for her to join him. As they passed the candy counter, Eden glanced at the selection for Good & Plenty but found the store to be lacking.

She let out a little growl of frustration.

"You okay?" Thomas turned to look at her, his eyes going straight to her stomach.

She giggled. "Yes, just pregnant and craving something I can't seem to find anywhere."

He smiled so wide she was certain the warmth of it would melt her into the floor. "I've got an extra package of donuts. Marge is holding the groceries until I'm finished up here."

Eden wasn't sure how to respond to that. He'd obviously paid attention to her purchase since he'd helped her get chocolate covered troublemakers down from the shelf. "Those were my second choice, not what I really wanted, but an alternative to the little pink and white black licorice candies I crave like a crack addict." She was almost embarrassed by her confession. She'd heard of plenty of cravings but no one she knew needed that box of candy almost as badly as she needed water, sleep, and sunshine.

"Good & Plenty. I haven't seen those in a life-time, but I'm sure Doc can order them."

"Like I said, I'll be on my way and out of your hair."

Thomas shook his head. "Let's decide on the next move after dinner. If you won't eat for you then at least eat for the baby."

She could never argue that logic. There was a lot she wouldn't do for herself and a great deal she'd do for others. It's how she'd gotten in this position in the first place.

"All right. You drive a hard bargain, Mr.—?"

"Cross. My name is Thomas Cross, but my friends call me Thomas."

"Are we friends now?" Something told her that being friends with Thomas would be an honor. What man picked a woman up off the street and carried her to the doctor? Then she remembered that Thomas was a fireman, so he probably did it out of a sense of duty rather than kindness.

"Let's make that happen. A person can't have

too many friends. Now how about that fried chicken?"

At the mention of food, her stomach growled.

They both let loose a laugh.

"You kids be safe," Agatha called from behind the counter.

Eden looked at the sweet older woman who Doctor Parker called Lovey and wondered if a man would ever love her enough to give her a nickname.

Thomas tucked Porkchop into the front seat of Eden's car and promised the cat they'd be back soon. His hand went to the small of her back as he led her into the diner. She immediately liked the place. The jukebox in the corner lit up the space even though it was silent.

Stepping into Maisey's was like stepping into a scene from *Grease*. She half expected to see the clientele moving around in poodle skirts and saddle shoes. Instead, a sandy blonde bounced on her Keds towards them.

"Hey, Thomas, you here for the blue plate special?" She followed them to a nearby booth.

"Hey." He looked at Eden. "Fried chicken, mashed potatoes and gravy and green beans. Are you in?"

The waitress scribbled his order down and looked at Eden. "You must be Eden. Doc called and said you'd be coming by. Told Ben to cut down on the salt for your meal."

Eden's eyes grew big. "Wow, news travels fast."

"My name is Riley, and I can tell you news in Aspen Cove goes from zero to sixty in about four seconds, but the people here mean well."

"So far, everyone has been wonderful to me."

"What's the point in being anything else? Will that be two blue plate specials?"

Eden nodded. "Sounds like it. One with less salt. Doctors orders. Can I have a glass of water please?"

"You got it."

Riley disappeared into the back of the restaurant, which left Eden alone with Thomas in the booth. He looked at her for a moment and then frowned.

"Geez, Eden, I'm sorry. I didn't consider your condition when I chose the booth. Let's move to a table where you'll be more comfortable."

She looked at him like he'd sprouted a single unicorn horn. "Um, are you sure? I mean, I can make do here." Her sister would have never thought to consider her needs but here was a man who had. Her world was topsy-turvy. She could have landed anywhere but happened to land in a slice of heaven.

Thomas was already out of the booth and offering her his hand. He walked her a few feet away and pulled out a chair. The simple gesture brought tears to her eyes.

He watched her swipe one away.

"I'm going to put a quarter in the jukebox. Any requests? It's all fifties music."

"Not really my era, so anything is fine." She watched him walk away. Her eyes went straight to his fine-fitting jeans. The way his denim hugged his muscled thighs and curved perfectly over the globes of his ass.

Eden really needed to focus on the problems at hand rather than create new ones. It was silly to fantasize over a man she could never have. She had to remember the way he'd looked at her the first time he'd seen she was pregnant. She wasn't sure what she'd seen in his expression, but she got the distinct impression it wasn't happiness, and it certainly wasn't attraction. He'd responded to her in the same way she responded to bees or wasps. She cut a wide berth around them, hoping she wouldn't get stung.

While he leaned over the jukebox, she pulled out her phone and dialed her mother. There was a sixteen-hour difference, which meant her mom was probably up and drinking her morning coffee.

The trill of an overseas ring echoed in her ear.

She'd keep it short so she wasn't forced into debtors' prison for a call.

"How's the trip going?" her mother answered. She never answered with a hello. It was always straight to the heart of the matter.

"I'm stalled a few hours outside of Denver."

"Car trouble? I told you to get a tune up."

"Mom, I can't afford a tune-up. The car is fine, but I had a medical emergency."

There was a moment of silence. "The baby?"

"Is fine, and I'm fine. Well, fine for now. Turns out my blood pressure is really high, and I've pulled a muscle in my stomach that sent me to my knees. The doctor here in town wants me to stay until the baby arrives, but I can't."

She could see her mother gnawing on her lip in her mind. It was always how she worked out her problems. "Does your sister know?"

"No, she's no longer privy to my health updates." Eden could feel her blood pressure rise. Could feel the heat of anger flush her cheeks. "I have nothing to say to her. I can't believe she told me she didn't want the baby."

Eden didn't realize she'd raised her voice but obviously she had by the heads that turned her direction, including Thomas's. He punched in a few numbers and walked back toward her when the music began. "Chances Are" played through the speaker.

"I've got to go, but I'll text and let you know what my plans are."

"You should stay put, Eden. I don't want anything to happen to my baby while you're having someone else's."

"Did it ever occur to you, Mom, that either way this was your grandchild?"

"What are you saying? Are you keeping the baby?"

"I'm not saying anything, and no, I'm not. How would that work out? Single mom. No job. No money. No hope. Talk to you later." She hung up the phone at the same time Thomas took his seat. Seconds later, Riley swung by to drop off two blue plate specials and two glasses of water.

Nothing was said for the first half of their dinner until Thomas broke the silence.

"The way I see it is you're in a predicament."

Eden let out a laugh. "You think?"

He cocked his head to the side. "I meant with your current health situation."

She looked down. "It's all related."

"You've been advised by a good doctor to stay put. I've been asked to lend a hand because I have a single-story rancher." He pushed his potatoes around his plate. "I'm on shift at the station several days a week so my house is vacant during that time. In all honesty, it's not that much of an inconvenience to me."

Each word came out as if it pained him. Why was it that she could see past his lies but could never see her sister's?

With her fork gripped in her hand, she took a bite of the green beans. The table was low compared to her stomach. Who needed a table when she had a belly that served as one? On any given day she could balance her food on top and shovel it directly into her mouth.

She quietly contemplated his offer. There was no doubt she was in a pickle. A couple of hours was all she'd driven when her back seized up, along with her bladder. How was she supposed to make it another three thousand miles in her condition? Add to that a freak storm and it was like the universe was screaming at her to stay put.

"I appreciate your offer, but I hate to impose. Surely, there's got to be a place nearby that I can stay. A hotel in the next town over, maybe?" How fast would her meager savings dwindle if she was forced to pay per night? The check from her sister still sat uncashed. When Suzanne was paying for the birth of her baby, it seemed reasonable, but now that she no longer wanted the child, it didn't seem right.

Eden had never wanted money to have the baby. It was a gift. Having thought about it for hours on end, she now wondered if the whole situation went back to her desire to have a lasting relationship with a woman who'd barely given her the time of day. They were worlds apart in every way. More than a decade separated them in age, but that wasn't where the differences started or stopped.

Suzanne was driven by something that Eden didn't understand. Her sister would walk across fire or find someone else to do it so she'd get what she wanted. This time it was Eden who would bear the heat and the blisters and the scars of Suzanne's desires. How many people had come before her? Now that she thought about it, her sister was an island. There weren't many friends knocking down her door for coffee dates and girls' nights out. Suzanne was singularly focused on herself, and that didn't leave much room for anyone else.

"You okay?"

She shook her head. There was no way she'd tell him her thoughts. To tell him the truth would only make her look as stupid as she felt. In what world had she thought that Suzanne would make a great mother?

"Yes, I was thinking about what towns were

close enough that I could see about a room, so I don't impose on anyone."

"Really, Eden, lodging is expensive, and I would assume a person in your situation would need to conserve her resources."

It bit at her that he could see she wasn't in a position to not take his hospitality. "A woman in my position?"

"No offense, but you're leaving something or someone. All your belongings are probably in your car. I've been in your car and there's not much in there. You're heading to Alaska to an aunt? That means you're turning to family. I'm not blind, and I'm far from dumb. You want to talk about it?"

"Nope. I can't argue with your logic, but you've got me all wrong." He didn't at all, but she hated that he looked on her with pity.

"Is that so? Tell me where I'm wrong."

"It's complicated. In hopes of keeping my blood pressure in check, I'm going to plead the fifth."

"Fair enough. Is it settled then? You'll be coming home with me."

Her shoulders sagged. What choice did she really have? "Yes, but I can pay you. I insist on paying you."

He chuckled. "There's no need. I pay the same for my house whether you're there or not."

"Are you all this nice, or have I only met the cream of the crop in town?"

Thomas shrugged. "I can't speak for everyone, but I can say from my experience you can't go wrong with the people here. If you had to get stranded anywhere, this is the place to be."

They finished their dinners and Eden insisted on paying. It was the least she could do. When they walked to her car he asked if she'd like him to drive.

"Don't you have to drive your own vehicle?"

"No, I walked. I live up the road a few blocks." He pointed toward the west where the mountains created the perfect backdrop to the setting sun. "Let me run in and get my groceries, and I'll be right back. Do you need anything?"

"No, you've done enough." She watched him disappear into the store. He rushed back out as if he was afraid she'd climb into her car and take off.

She tossed him her keys and he caught them in his free hand. "You trust me?"

"Don't really have a choice now, do I?"

CHAPTER TEN

THOMAS

He pulled her car into the driveway and looked at his house from her perspective. He'd spent so much time working on the inside that he hadn't really considered the outside until today when he'd plucked weeds and straightened out the pickets.

"It doesn't look like much, but it's a work in progress."

"Oh no, it's great. It has a lot of charm. Have you lived here long?"

He chuckled. "Feels like a lifetime but in all honesty, I just bought the place."

"Umm, I didn't ask, but do you have a wife or a girlfriend? It could be awkward bringing home a stray."

The light rumble in his chest turned into laughter. "Nope, no wife and no girlfriend. Not looking for one."

"Right, okay." Her cheeks blushed pink. "Are you okay with Porkchop?"

He turned to look at the cat, who had been moved to the backseat to make room for Eden.

"I wasn't certain at first, but it looks like we've come to an understanding." He opened the door and rushed around to get hers. "Let me show you around, and then I'll come back and get your things."

"Oh no, I can get my stuff." She lifted to her feet, but he could tell she was still feeling the strain on her muscles.

"Nope. My mom would be so disappointed in me if I allowed you to carry anything. She'd reach over several states to give me a wallop across the head."

He offered her his hand and helped her to her feet. He liked the way her palm fit inside his. It reminded him of a time when his heart was open, and his life was different.

In Aspen Cove he rarely locked his door. There didn't seem to be a point. Every street had an old-timer that kept an eye on things. His gate guard was Mr. Larkin, who was already peeking his head out the door.

"You work fast, my boy. I didn't know they came mostly baked."

"Go back inside, Peter." Thomas opened the front door and rushed Eden inside. "Sorry about that. He's old and lonely. I offered him a beer today. Maybe that's like feeding a stray cat or a raccoon. I fear he thinks we're best friends now."

"He seems harmless."

They stood in his entry, which was really just the side of his living room. The older bungalow type homes were made for working class people. They didn't have fancy foyers or grand entrances.

"This is the living room." He walked her straight ahead to the kitchen. "Help yourself to anything you want. Right now, there's not much in the way of food but as soon as I unload my groceries, what's mine is yours."

"I'll be happy to provide meals for us."

"You cook?" He hadn't given her contribution much thought. He had no expectations of Eden except that she made it to the end of her pregnancy in good health.

"I love to cook."

He shook his head. "I don't expect you to cook but if you're cooking for yourself and there happens to be enough for two ..." He left it at that and moved her down the hallway. "The first room on the left is the master bedroom." He looked around and realized that he'd have to give her his bed. He only had one bed in the house and he couldn't expect her to sleep on the couch. "You'll be staying in here."

"No, this is your room. I can stay in the spare room." She peeked her head out the door down the hallway where there were additional rooms.

"That's all good in theory, but you'll see the problem soon enough." He moved ahead of her to the first door. "This will be my office as soon as I have time to patch the holes in the walls and fix the electrical." He flipped on the switch to make a point that there was no power to the room. He moved to the next door, which was a bathroom. "I'll use this bathroom." He walked to the last room. "This is ..." What did he say ... his man cave? "It's a media room."

She looked inside and then glanced over her shoulder toward the living room. "What would you call the place where we entered?"

"The living room?"

"Okay," she said with a soft upwards lilt to her voice. She peeked back inside. "Oh, I see, this television is bigger than the one out there."

"Cute and observant."

"Excuse me?"

"I said you've got a good eye. That screen in there is eighty-four inches. This one ... well, it's bigger and you know, they say size matters."

He wanted to superglue his lips shut. Why the hell did he tell her that?

"Apparently it does as far as televisions go."

As he looked down at her, he could see her hair was the color of a full moon. An almost angelic white. There were touches of pink that weaved through, as if she'd been dipped in cotton candy. Her eyes were like a good scotch, a golden amber brown that lit up when she smiled.

"Let me get your things so you can get moved in." He turned to walk away, but she laid her hand on his arm.

"Thomas, I don't know what to say. Thank you seems inadequate."

He said nothing. He simply looked at her, gave her a nod and rushed down the hallway and outside.

His heart raced so fast he was certain it would explode in his chest. How in the hell had he come face to face with his biggest fear?

In his head, he heard his mother's voice. "What you don't face head-on will always chase you." Sarah's betrayal hadn't only hurt him but his parents too. They had been ecstatic about becoming grandparents. Deep inside, he knew that was part of the reason they'd moved to Florida. Seeing Sarah and her daughter, whom she'd named Heather, would have been like opening a wound. Peeling off a scab each time. It was the main reason he'd left Silver Springs. As much as he'd tried to avoid her, there were plenty of times they'd crossed paths and he wasn't a masochist.

He reached in for Porkchop and the bag of groceries. It took him three more trips to get her belongings, the litter box, and the cat tree that was wedged into the back.

When he made the last trip, he found her standing in front of his bed. "If I take your room, where will you sleep?"

"I've got the couch."

She shook her head. The soft curls framing her face bounced with the movement.

"No way. I'm not taking your bed. I'll sleep on the couch. I'll fit, you won't."

He lifted his brows. He didn't want to point out that while her height was an advantage, her girth was not. Not that she was huge. She was a healthy pregnant weight. All belly and boobs. He mentally chastised himself for having noticed the latter, but hell if he could miss them.

"Let's give it a try and see what happens.

You'll be more comfortable in my bed and it's your lucky day because today was sheet changing day." He pointed to the pile of laundry on the floor in the corner.

"I'd say I've hit the lotto with my stop here in Aspen Cove."

Before he could reply, a howl came from the living room. "Is that the cat?"

"Oh, my goodness, she probably needs her litter box." Eden rushed past him, leaving him in a cloud of her sweet scent. He wasn't sure if it was floral or sugar. She smelled like pancakes on a Sunday morning or a flower shop full of blooms. It was an intoxicating blend that made his entire body respond.

I need to get out more. The fact that a pregnant stranger could make him hard was testament to the dry spell he'd encountered. It wasn't because of lack of offers. It was because of lack of interest. No one caught his eye.

By the time he got to the living room. Eden was filling up the litter box and letting out the cat. Thomas had never been a pet kind of guy. He spent too much time at the station and felt it would have been irresponsible to own an animal he couldn't devote his time to. If he were honest with himself it was probably the number one reason his relationship with Sarah failed. More than half of his time was spent on shift at the fire station. That left her a lot of hours on her hands. It never crossed his mind when she called and said she was working late that she was actually on the couch in her boss's office. It gave new meaning to the position of cocktail waitress to him.

"Let me get that." He took the heavy box of litter from her hands. "Aren't litter boxes dangerous to pregnant women?"

She looked up and smiled. "Cute and intelligent."

They both laughed.

"I tie a scarf around my face when I change the litter. So far it's not been an issue."

He picked up the box and carried it to the unfinished room. "How about we set up the kitty bathroom in here? I'll take over as the official pooper scooper from here on out. I don't want you anywhere near it while you're on my watch."

"Who are you?"

"I'm no one really."

He had no warning before she threw herself into his arms. "You're wrong. You're everything to me. You have no idea."

The curve of her stomach pushed low against him. Naturally, his arms wrapped around her. Tugging her tightly to his body, he rubbed her back and leaned his chin on the top of her head. "It will be okay, Eden."

She said nothing for a long moment before she took a big breath and stepped back. "It will have to be, won't it?"

He emptied a couple of his drawers for her and shifted his clothes in the closet to make room for hers. It was an odd feeling to have dresses hang next to his pants, but it was also comforting. He'd been alone for so long. He hadn't realized or wanted to admit how lonely he'd become.

It should have been painfully obvious when he'd been excited to have the octogenarian over for a beer. When had his life gotten so out of whack? That was easy math. Five years ago, when he found out the baby wasn't his.

"The master bath is remodeled. The shower has jets so when your back is sore that would be a good place to go." He moved toward the en suite and showed her where the towels were and pulled out an empty drawer and told her it was hers.

"Do you talk to your mom often?"

It was a strange out of the blue question. "Sure, we talk a few times a month. Why?"

She stared up at him with a soft expression. "Next time you talk to her, tell her she should be proud of the son she raised. You're a good man, Thomas."

"How would you know?"

"Look at what you've done for me." She grabbed his hand and pressed it to the top of her rippling belly. "Even the baby says so."

His first instinct was to pull his hand away as if he'd been burned but he couldn't because he was mesmerized by the strength of the kicks.

"Wow, you've got a soccer player in there. Does that hurt?"

She moved his hand around as if following the baby's movement. "Sometimes, but not now. It's like he or she is telling me thanks for dinner. Pretty soon everything will settle down for the night."

He let his hand drop from her stomach. "Thank you for sharing that."

She let her head fall. "It's all I really have to share."

He leaned down in front of her. "Hey little person, you've got a good mommy."

"How would you know?"

She'd repeated his words.

"What you're doing? It's the ultimate commitment. You're sharing your body twenty-four-seven to bring a baby into this world. You think I'm a good person because I'm sharing my house with you for a month. I pale in comparison." He stood straight and walked out of the room.

He didn't see her the rest of the night, but he heard her. At first, he thought it was the cat, but when he put his ear to the door, his heart tumbled into his stomach. Eden wept for hours while he stood by not knowing what to do and hating himself for it.

CHAPTER ELEVEN

EDEN

She stretched her arms and let out a yawn. There was no doubt that when she ventured into the bathroom and looked in the mirror, she'd see the effects of last night's emotional breakdown. How she hated herself for being so weak. Despite the negative turn of events in her life, her number one focus was delivering a healthy baby. Crying for hours wasn't a good habit.

She rolled to her feet and padded across the hardwood floors to the bathroom. One look at her puffy eyes doubled her remorse. Not only would she feel bad for the baby, but everyone who would come into contact with her today. Her appearance was frightful.

With a hand on her stomach she turned on the taps to start her morning routine. She was running out of time to make a plan. A plan that started with finding a job, investigating options for her unborn child, and somehow paying Thomas back for his hospitality.

Her circumstances could be deemed unlucky, and in many ways, they were, but how she'd rolled into Aspen Cove was a mystery that only a craving for candy could explain. How lucky was she that she'd found a place that was willing to help a stranger?

Fifteen minutes later she opened the door to the bedroom confident enough that when she encountered Thomas, she wouldn't frighten him. Her hair was brushed, her makeup applied, and she was dressed and presentable.

The house was quiet. She ventured down the hallway to find the couch empty. The only thing signifying anyone had slept there was a neatly folded comforter and a pillow stacked on top. Her heart squeezed at his chivalrous behavior. Men nowadays weren't raised to open doors, let a woman go first, or give up their bed.

Most would throw out a smile and wish that something happened to improve her lot in life right before they walked away. Thomas Cross was different.

"Thomas?" she called out. "Are you here?" She listened for any sound, but the only response was Porkchop tearing down the hallway and sliding on the slick wooden surface until she collided with her ankles.

Her plaintive meows were her way of telling Eden she was starving.

"You're so predictable." She squatted down to give the cat a scratch between the ears. She'd given up bending over months ago. Her center of gravity was off and invariably she almost always took a stumble forward.

"Let's go." With the cat strutting behind her, they entered the kitchen where to her surprise she found a note taped to the coffee pot.

Good morning Eden,

I made you a pot of decaf knowing that most pregnant women avoid caffeine. If that's not the case I apologize for my assumption. Help yourself to anything you need and don't forget that Doc Parker wants to see you sometime today.

Should you need me, please don't hesitate to call. I'm pulling twelve-hour shifts this week at the fire station but can swing by and pick you up if you need a ride.

Thomas

She ran her fingers over the neat handwriting.

The man had made her decaf and left his phone number on the bottom of the sheet.

While a ride sounded marvelous, there was no way she would impose on him. Giving up his house was enough. There had to be a way to pay it forward.

She reached into the paper bag of cat supplies and took out a can of cat food. Porkchop danced around her ankles like she hadn't eaten in days when she'd been fed last night. In fact, a bowl of dry food sat untouched in the corner of the kitchen next to a bowl of water—no doubt filled by Thomas.

"Poor man, he had no idea what helping us would turn into." With the cat taken care of, she picked up her purse and headed into the sunshine. She'd considered shoehorning herself into the driver's seat of her car, but a walk sounded wonderful and no doubt would be good for her health as well as her disposition.

She remembered the route back into town. It was just a couple of blocks. As the sun kissed her cheeks, she glanced around the charming town with intersecting street names like Rose and Hyacinth and Pansy. The mountains were like arms hugging her from two sides and in the distance, the sparkling glass surface of a lake peeked between properties.

It took her fifteen minutes to get to Main Street. Not because of the distance but because of the distractions. There were too many quaint houses. Some fully restored and some near ruin but all telling a story about the town and how what once was downtrodden would soon be restored. She hoped her own story could have a similar trajectory.

She gripped the handle of the clinic door and pushed it open. The bell from above jingled and Doc's Lovey lifted her head from the newspaper.

"Oh, Eden, so glad to see you. How are you feeling?" She moved toward the nearby staircase as she spoke.

"I'm okay. I got a good night's sleep and a nice walk over here."

The older woman held up a finger and hollered, "Paul, your patient arrived."

Eden thought she heard him answer something like *Thank you, Lovey,* but she couldn't be sure.

"Let me take you back to the office. If you've forgotten, I'm Agatha."

"Doc calls you Lovey."

She blushed. "He does and I love it, but it would be weird if you called me that."

"Agatha it is."

As soon as Eden took a seat in the chair in the corner, Doc walked inside.

"How's the little mama? Was Thomas accommodating?"

"He's wonderful." It was funny how swoony her voice sounded, but the words were true. "He's been great. I feel bad because he gave me his room."

Doc shook his head.

She wasn't certain what that meant. Was it because she should have spent the night on the couch or something else?

"Serves him right. He's got three bedrooms and one bed. That sounds like piss poor planning to me."

Some unrestrainable need to defend Thomas surfaced. "It's his house. He can do as he likes. His media room is impressive."

"How many televisions does one man need?"

She laughed. "Apparently two. Massively big ones."

Doc checked her blood pressure and gave her a frown. "No salt. Get some rest. Eat healthy. I'll see you tomorrow."

She took that to mean that there was no change. "Do I check out at the front? I'd like to pay you for yesterday and today." If her pressure hadn't spiked yet it would now. The unknown of what his fees would be made her insides twist. While she still had the check from her sister, it was supposed to cover the birth of the baby. The amount she gave her might be sufficient, but she doubted it. Given the circumstances, the money felt wrong and dirty and she wouldn't cash the damn check unless she absolutely had to.

"No charge."

She did a double take. "Excuse me?"

"I said no charge. If you argue with me, I'll charge you double."

She shook her head. "Isn't nothing times two still nothing?"

Doc led her to the front door. "I knew you were a smart one." He pulled the door open. "You have enough problems. You don't need to borrow more. I'm happy to help where I can."

So overwhelmed with his kindness, she stood on her tiptoes and kissed his weathered cheek. "Thanks, Doc."

Porkchop had been fed, but she had not. She'd thrown back a cup of coffee before she dashed out the door and now her appetite was rearing its ugly head. She lifted her nose and followed the smell of bacon to the diner.

Inside, she wandered over to the same table

where she and Thomas had shared dinner last night. Only this time a woman with a sleek blond bob came to the table. Her name tag read Maisey. No doubt the owner of the diner.

"You must be Eden."

"News travels fast." If she wasn't so big, she would have crawled under the table.

"My niece waited on you and Thomas last night. She's also Luke's girl so ..."

"Luke?" She had no idea who that was.

"Luke is the fire chief."

"Oh." She put two and two together fast. "Your niece is lovely."

Maisey laughed. "I'll keep her." She leaned against the table. "What will it be? I hear Doc wants you on a low salt plan so no breakfast meats but how about pancakes or oatmeal and fresh fruit?"

The little one gave her an internal beating that said any food would be appreciated. "Oatmeal and fruit would be wonderful."

"Coming up." Several minutes later, Maisey was back with a big glass of milk and a smaller glass of juice. "Need your vitamins D and C. Drink up."

"Thank you." She sipped the milk and looked around the place. Was it always this slow or only because school had started back up? Did they close in the winter and if so where would the locals eat? She had so many unanswered questions about the town. Having grown up in larger cities, she wasn't used to the nuances of small-town life, but if they were all like Aspen Cove, she couldn't figure out why anyone would want to live anywhere else. If she were truly going to have a baby, this would be the perfect place to raise a child.

The thunk of the bowl on the table took her out of her thoughts.

"Anything else, sweetheart?"

"Um…" Did she dare ask? Did she dare not? She had limited resources and needed a job. "Yes. Do you have or know of anyone who … needs help? I could really use a job. Since Doc Parker doesn't want me traveling in my advanced condition, I'm stuck here without resources."

Maisey pulled out the chair across from her. "Oh honey, I'd give you a job in a second, but working here won't be good for your health. You come talk to me once that baby arrives, and I'll hook you up."

An unexpected tear slipped from Eden's eye. It was silly to cry, but she was moved by the kindness and moved by desperation. "Okay, I'll figure something out then. I have experience. I know what the work is like."

Maisey's face softened. "Then you know that it's not the best option right now."

She couldn't argue. The last few weeks had been arduous, and at the end of her shift everything hurt. The aches and pains had barely gone away before the next shift began.

"Thank you for your consideration. If you know anyone who can use the help of a very pregnant woman, I'd be grateful for the information."

Maisey rubbed her chin between her thumb and finger. "You eat, I'll be right back." Maisey moved out of her seat like a bullet from a pistol and raced out the front door.

The first bite of oatmeal made her nose scrunch. "Needs salt," she said to no one. She tossed in the fresh berries served in a bowl on the side and a splash of milk and things got a lot better.

The door opened and Maisey came in with a woman pushing a double stroller.

"This is Charlie Whatley." Maisey pulled out the seat she'd been sitting in and moved the stroller beside it. "You two need to have a talk. You have a lot in common." Maisey stared at Eden's stomach before she walked away.

The pretty woman sat down across from her. "Hi, Eden. Maisey tells me you're looking for a job."

"I am. I know it seems odd since I'm obviously pregnant and close to my due date, but I've found myself in a predicament. While I can't control many factors, a job would solve a lot of my problems." She couldn't help but lean forward to look into the stroller, where two little boys were sleeping. A dusting of brown hair covered their heads and angelic bowed lips puffed out air in slow rhythmic breaths.

"This must be my lucky week. I could use some help."

Eden was certain she'd heard wrong. "Did you say you need help?"

Charlie pointed to the babies. "They're a handful but a blessing. I worked until the day I delivered so I know you can do it. All I need is someone to answer phones for a few hours in the morning and schedule appointments for the afternoon." She smiled as she looked at Eden's stomach. "When you deliver, you can bring the baby to work with you."

Her heart picked up its pace. Was it because she had a job or because Charlie assumed that she'd keep the baby? Could she? It was the first time she'd considered that a possibility.

"What kind of job is this?"

Charlie laughed. "I'm the town veterinarian.

Doc Parker is my father, and I run the animal clinic next to his place."

"Oh, your father is amazing and so nice."

"He is, but he's also a meddler, so watch out for him."

"I'm already the recipient of his kindness, but in truth he's been more of a help than a hindrance."

"He's a father to many." There was a look of sadness in her eyes. "As his daughter it took me a long time to realize how good he really is." She laid her hands on the table. "You want to start tomorrow at nine?"

"Really?" She knew she should have asked about the pay and hours, but whatever she would make was certainly more than the nothing she was bringing in now.

Having a job meant she'd be out of Thomas's house and out of his hair. It also meant she could contribute as a way to thank him for his generosity.

"Yep. Let's do four hours a day and fifteen dollars an hour."

"Wow, that's a lot for answering phones."

"It's a lot of calls. A lot of scheduling and some of our clients"—she swirled her finger near her ear—"they like to talk about everything for a long time. I'd pay you twice as much to talk to Mrs.

Brown if I could, but that's the most I can afford right now."

"It's too much, but I'll take it."

She rose and gave Charlie a hug. She'd been giving a lot of hugs lately. If she wasn't certain she was awake, she'd bet her life she was dreaming. Somehow, she'd found herself in a storybook instead of a town.

CHAPTER TWELVE

THOMAS

Thomas rubbed the chrome with a soft towel, bringing the trim on the rig to a diamond-like sparkle. It wasn't their normal Saturday shining session. That had been yesterday, but he needed to get his mind off Eden, and how he'd listened to her cry for hours last night.

"You planning on rubbing a hole through that today or do you think it will take you until next week?" Luke asked.

"Just keeping busy." He tossed the towel to the concrete floor and climbed down from the truck. "You need me for something?"

"Why don't you and I head over to Copper Creek and get supplies? James and Jacob have cleared out the cupboards and they're telling Maisey I'm starving them to death."

Thomas chuckled. "They both have hollow legs. I don't think they're ever full. Maybe you should take one of them so they can't blame you for not buying enough."

Luke bent over and swiped up the cloth and tossed it into a nearby trash can. "Neither of them looked like they need a break. You've got something on your mind, and it's written all over your face."

He shook his head at his boss. "If it's written all over my face then there's no reason to talk about it. I'm a walking billboard."

Luke tossed him the keys to the company truck. "You drive, and I'll listen. Something tells me it all started with a pregnant woman."

His heart took a dive straight to his steel-toe boots. Luke couldn't have known how close to the mark he was. While he was referring to Eden, Thomas knew it all started with Sarah.

They hopped inside the truck and headed to Copper Creek.

"You sure those two won't burn down the station?"

Luke laughed. "They might, but at least they're trained to put the fire out."

Thomas glanced in the rearview mirror to catch Jacob shooting a basketball into the newly installed hoop. They all thought it would be a great idea. It was good exercise and it created a place where the locals interacted in friendly games with the crew.

One of the things he loved most about Aspen Cove was the sense of community. His thoughts went back to Eden. She'd been there a day and yet everyone knew her, or about her and people were stepping up to the plate to do what they could to help. He'd walked out the door this morning and found a box of baby clothes on the porch. He had no idea who they were from, but he set them in the garage and would give them to Eden when he got home.

How many casseroles had been delivered when he bought the house? For the first week, he'd walked out to find flower bulbs and paint for his fence. He wasn't sure if it was a gift of kindness or a hint to get things done.

He turned onto the highway that connected the towns.

"What's got you frowning like a kid who dropped their ice cream cone?" Luke asked.

"I'm not frowning."

"Bullshit, you've got a crater the size of a

canyon creasing your forehead. Are you unhappy that Doc bullied you into taking in a stray?"

That was exactly how Eden had described herself yesterday. He made an attempt to relax his brows. The strain in his muscles gave him a headache.

"The timing is inconvenient. I'm trying to get the house finished by the first snowfall. All I want to do during my days off is watch football and Netflix."

"And she's stopping you?"

He shook his head. "No, but I can't paint because she's pregnant, the fumes are dangerous. I don't want to make a lot of dust or noise. I'm single for a reason."

There was a moment of silence. "What is that reason?"

He turned on the radio. "Another time maybe."

Luke turned it off. "No diversions. There's no time like the present. Besides, you're my friend, and it's time we got to know each other better."

"You want to have a sleepover and roast weenies?"

"We have sleepovers a few times a month at the station and we never roast weenies. Now tell me, is it Eden?"

"I just don't get her. She's eight months preg-nant and alone. What man leaves his woman alone?"

Luke heaved a sigh. "Not all women need a man to have a baby."

Thomas chanced a look at his friend. "Every woman needs a man to have a baby or at least his sperm. There's a man out there who's going to be a father, and if he knows and isn't taking care of her then he's an asshole. If he doesn't know because she's been dishonest, then she's the asshole."

"Does she seem like a dishonest person?"

"No, but who does? Women lie all the time." Each time he thought about Sarah he was gutted.

Luke fidgeted with the air vents as if the con-versation was making him uncomfortably warm.

That would be fine for Thomas since he didn't want to talk about any of it anyway.

"Tell me about her."

He shrugged. "She's pretty and easy to talk to but she's hiding something." He thought about telling him how she'd cried all night, but somehow that seemed wrong. If Eden wanted everyone to know her misery, she'd cry in public, not hide in his room with her face buried in his pillow. "I asked her if she wanted to talk about her situation and she clammed up."

"She doesn't know you. Obviously, if she's heading somewhere in the late stages of her pregnancy, things aren't going her way. Let her warm up to you. Give her a reason to trust you."

"Why can't she just tell me the truth? I'm opening my house to her."

"Opening your house is far different from opening your heart. Don't expect something from her that you wouldn't give yourself."

"What? I'm open."

"No, you're not. I know you've been hurt, but hell, man, haven't we all? It's how we grow and define what we want and what we're willing to put up with. Who the hell shredded your heart?"

The only people who knew about Sarah and the baby were his parents and his team in Silver Springs. Did he dare tell Luke? Moving to Aspen Cove was his way of leaving it all behind, but had he? It was still a fresh memory even though years had passed. He felt the betrayal like a dull rusty knife nicking at his heart. All he had to see was a pregnant woman or a baby and he bled a little bit more. It was death by a thousand cuts. Lately, with all the marriages and babies, he'd been hemorrhaging.

"You want to know?" He lifted a brow and glanced at Luke. "I had a fiancée named Sarah. I loved her more than I loved anything. She was pregnant with our first child—a girl we were going to name Heather after the pink flowers that Sarah loved so much."

Luke rubbed his jaw. "What happened? Did something bad happen?"

"Oh yeah, something really bad happened. I watched as my daughter was born. Cut her umbilical cord and kissed my soon-to-be wife." He remembered looking at her with such awe and love. Sarah refused to get married while she was pregnant. She wanted the dress and the flowers and the crowd of people buying her too many toasters. When he looked at her in that moment, he knew soon he'd make her his forever. "God, man, it was the most beautiful moment. My life was perfect. Then it all turned to shit when I found out Heather wasn't mine."

"Oh hell. I'm sorry, man. That must be incredibly hard to have Eden in your house. Does Doc know?"

"No, you're the first person I've told, and I want it to stay between us. I don't want to be seen as the guy who was cheated on." How crazy was it that somehow her cheating made him feel inadequate? It didn't matter how many times he tried to convince himself that he'd been enough, the fact that she'd gone looking for something else, somewhere else, meant he hadn't been.

"I'm not saying a word. All I'm going to do is caution you. Don't make Eden pay for Sarah's sins. Things aren't always how our minds spin them. There are a lot of reasons she could be pregnant and alone."

"Enlighten me."

Luke thought for a second. "Maybe she wants to be a single mother."

"Nope. I don't believe that for a second."

"Maybe she bats for the other team and bought swimmies at the local sperm bank."

"Unlikely. She doesn't seem like the type who would have that kind of money. It's not like she's pushing the edge of her biological clock. She's twenty-eight."

"She could be a widow, or an abuse victim. It could have been a one-night stand. Who knows, maybe she is running away or keeping the baby from its father, but there would be a reason, and don't you think you should find out before you rush to judgment?"

He had a point. "You're right." He pulled in the parking lot where they did their bulk shopping. He didn't have Eden's trust because he hadn't earned it, but he would. Something told him she needed someone to count on and while he wasn't sure he was that person, he'd have to be until she found another more qualified.

The first place he headed was to the candy aisle where he found a case of her favorites. Yep, he'd earn Eden's trust one pink and white candy at a time.

CHAPTER THIRTEEN

EDEN

Thomas called yesterday afternoon and told her they had been asked to help with an out of control fire on the other side of the mountain so he wouldn't be home. While he owed her no excuses for his whereabouts, she was appreciative that he kept her in the loop.

The day alone gave her time to think about her situation and get used to her surroundings. Thomas's house was pure man. Everything was black, gray and white. There wasn't the slightest bit of color except for his underwear and T-shirts piled in the corner of his room. Those were pink.

She'd carelessly run a red sweater with her whites not too long ago, so she knew exactly what to do and had the product she needed to fix the problem.

Since today was her first day at her new job, she'd risen early, threw in a load of wash in hopes that Thomas wouldn't be upset with her for touching his belongings, and sat down for a cup of decaf coffee. Oh, how she looked forward to the day when she could have a double shot latte.

A quick thump to her ribcage reminded her that while she felt alone, she wasn't alone. "Hey, little one. Are you happy?"

A lump stuck in her throat. She was bringing a child into this world. He or she should have parents that were over the moon about the arrival and yet the only one excited was her. She had to admit that she dreamed on more than one occasion about how it would feel to be able to keep the baby. She always consoled herself that she'd be a huge part of its life.

Thinking that she would have to turn her baby over to a stranger made her heart ache.

"Damn you, Suzanne."

Her mother had warned her. She'd told her that Suzanne wasn't ready to be a parent, but Eden thought at forty years old, her sister couldn't wait much longer if she wanted a child. Brady seemed to be on board but in hindsight, he gave Suzanne whatever she wanted just to shut her up.

No wonder their marriage fell apart. It was never a compromise. The poor man didn't stand a chance when her sister set her eyes on him. She was like a bulldozer and everyone around her like hot tar. She ran them over and pressed them into place.

All those years she'd looked up to her. Hell, she wanted to be her. Wanted to be seen by her. Now she never wanted to see her again.

Eden put her empty coffee mug in the dishwasher and picked up her purse before she headed out the door. Her plan was to stop by Doc Parker's for a blood pressure check before she started her new job.

She'd barely made it to the sidewalk when she saw the old man across the street heading for her.

"Hey there." He shuffled forward and crossed the street. "I'm Peter Larkin and you must be new in town."

She smiled. Mr. Larkin reminded her of her neighbor Mr. Schubert. She never thought she'd miss him, but he always had something nice to say. On occasion, he had a few not so nice things to say as well. Like when Mrs. Goff was making corned beef and cabbage and he swore it smelled like sewage.

"Yes, I'm ..." What did she say? That she was depending on the kindness of strangers because she'd made a bad choice? Having this baby wasn't a bad choice, it was simply an uneducated choice. Or a choice made without thoroughly weighing the outcome. "I'm passing through."

He looked over her shoulder to Thomas's house. "Is he the father?"

She shook her head. "No, he isn't."

Mr. Larkin's face pruned up. "Well damn, I thought maybe he'd been hiding you all along. You could do worse than Thomas."

"I'd give up a career in sales if that's your pitch."

"He's a good lad."

"I keep hearing that, and I'd agree. He's a good man." Or so she imagined since he'd taken her in without so much as a blink. "I've got to go. I'm starting a new job at the vet clinic."

He patted her back. "Good for you." Like everyone else, his eyes lowered to her stomach. "You got everything you need for that baby?"

She swallowed the lump in her throat. She wasn't ready to share her story. There was a level of embarrassment that came along with her situation. How had she judged someone so wrongly? How had she brought a child into this world without a solid plan? She reminded herself that she'd had a plan, but that had fallen through, and now she needed a different one.

"I'm getting it all together."

"Good to hear. I could rummage up a few things if you want some help. Just let me know what you're looking for. I have two bad habits. Loose women and garage sales."

She walked away laughing.

Agatha was standing behind the counter when she arrived. "Head on back, Eden. Lydia is already here. She can square you away."

She scanned the candy selection before she ventured back. If she was going to get her sugar fix it would have to be with an alternative or maybe she'd give up the habit altogether. The little one gave her a knee buckling kick. "I agree. What's life without an indulgence?"

Lydia saw her coming and ushered her straight into the exam room.

"How are you feeling today?"

"Feeling good and relieved." She'd called her aunt the day she got stranded in Aspen Cove and found out the storm was expected sooner. This morning she'd received a text. "Turns out my body stress was a blessing in disguise. I was heading to my aunt's in Alaska and an early storm hit. Enough snowfall to require chains."

"Wow, that is early. We probably won't see snow until October."

She slid onto the exam table and Doctor Covington took her blood pressure. "Looks a little better but it's not in the normal range yet. Your urine sample was fine. Are you under a lot of stress?"

She had been certain that Doc had told everyone her story. Hell, she'd let it all gush out of her like a geyser, but apparently, he took his oath of confidentiality to heart.

"I am. It's been an interesting few weeks." Her throat tightened and she was certain the tears would start any minute if she didn't get her emotions under control. "My life has taken a sharp detour."

Lydia laughed. "Oh, I know that detour. You know that story about how you have a path planned? Maybe you're going to Paris and then all of a sudden you end up in Singapore? Aspen Cove is my Singapore. I never expected to land here, but I did, and it's better than Paris could have been."

Lydia gave her the short version of her story about a cheating boyfriend, a lost job, and a goal that didn't meet her dreams once she'd met Wes. "I believe the universe has a plan for all of us." She helped Eden off the exam table. "I'd say Alaska wasn't in your plans."

She had a half hour before she was due at the vet clinic, so she popped into the bakery. Opening the door was like entering paradise.

"Mornin'," a little blonde said from behind the counter. "You must be Eden."

"I am."

"We have a muffin schedule here. Today is carrot cake Monday, but I also have cookies and brownies."

"A muffin would be great."

"I'm Katie." She pointed to a table underneath the wishing wall corkboard. "First muffin is on the house."

"I can pay for it." She rummaged through her purse for the wad of ones she had from her last shift at Rocco's.

"Nonsense. I give away more muffins than I sell." She pointed to the two boxes on the counter. "Those are for the fire department and the police department. Someone comes by each morning to pick them up." She plated a muffin and brought it around to where Eden had taken a seat.

"Thank you."

Katie plopped into the chair across from her. "Tell me about you?"

"Not much to tell. I'm Eden Webster. I'm a waitress usually, but today I'm starting a new job at the vet clinic."

"That Charlie is amazing. Not only does she take care of the town's animals, but I swear she's a dog whisperer. She whipped my Lab into shape. I wrote a wish on the board and the next day she was at my house."

"So you're a baker and a wish maker."

Katie looked up to the cork board. "It started out as something fun, but I've found out that around here, wishes do come true." She peeled a sticky note from the board and handed her a pen. "Give it a try. You never know what might happen." She hopped up. "I'll be in the back if you need me. Welcome to Aspen Cove, Eden."

She stared at the yellow piece of paper. She had a thousand and one wishes but her biggest wasn't for herself. All she wanted was for everything to work out for her baby, so she scribbled down a note to that effect and pinned it to the wall.

She finished her muffin and walked outside. Her heart rate picked up the nearer she got to the vet clinic. Anything that was new was stressing. She only hoped that it didn't adversely affect the baby. Considering her options, starving was a far worse fate than a sore back and sore feet.

Charlie was behind the counter when she arrived. Next to her was a handsome man and the twin's stroller.

"Hey, Eden. This is my husband Trig."

She looked at the couple with envy. There were couples who at once glance she knew were in love and Trig and Charlie had that glow about them despite the arrival of twins and no doubt their lack of sleep.

"Nice to meet you."

"Better to meet you," he said in a deep baritone voice. "You have no idea how grateful we are that you showed up in town." He leaned over and kissed his wife on the cheek and rolled the babies out the door.

"You guys are so cute together."

"He's pretty damn awesome."

"Have you been married long?"

Charlie chuckled. "Under a year. Funny thing was I didn't know if I loved him or loathed him until I almost lost him." She explained how Trig had lost the lower part of his leg in the war and got an infection that almost killed him. "It's funny how it comes down to the simplest things. In the end, life isn't all that complicated. We just make it that way."

Something about that statement threaded its way through Eden. Could her life be as simple as she wished it to be? The bigger question was, would she hate herself if she gave up the baby or hate herself more if she kept it and proved to be an inadequate mother?

The next two hours were spent learning the scheduling system. She paid close attention to her

new boss, but her mind kept returning to her situation. Her life was complicated, but did it have
to be?

Once her shift was complete, she walked into the corner store. Thomas had texted her to let her know he'd be returning to his home around six. He didn't want to startle her. Again, he owed her nothing and yet he kept her informed. That was not only thoughtful, but it gave her an idea of how to pay him back for some of his kindness.

CHAPTER FOURTEEN

THOMAS

Basil and oregano scented the air. Had he entered the wrong house? Thomas walked into the living room to find the books on his coffee table stacked, his remote controls laid out in order of size and the blanket and pillow he'd used the last night he slept there tucked into the corner out of the way.

The soft sound of music blended with the aroma of Italian cooking. Like a hook on a line, she reeled him in.

Unaware of his presence, she swayed to the music playing from her phone. An older song from the seventies or eighties about a lonely boy.

He crossed his arms and leaned against the doorframe and waited for her to notice she wasn't alone. While she danced and sang and stirred, he considered her plight and his own.

This exact scenario was his years ago. He'd come home and find Sarah in the kitchen. She never sang, but she danced from appliance to appliance until she'd twirl around and find him staring.

Those stares always got him in trouble because Sarah, like many women, had an increased libido while pregnant. Not that he minded. How many lunches had he come home for and never eaten a bite?

"Do you think Thomas will like this?" Her head fell, her hair, no doubt, creating a curtain in front of her face. "I don't want to overstep our boundaries, but he's been so kind."

He didn't want to get caught eavesdropping, so he stepped back a few feet trying to escape without notice but his stomach growled, and she whipped around to face him.

"Hey, Eden." He made his way into the kitchen, dropped his to-go coffee cup into the sink, and leaned on the counter. He pretended like he hadn't been staring at her for minutes. "That smells great. What are you cooking?"

Over her shoulder, a bubbly cauldron of pasta sauce simmered.

Her brown eyes stared into his. "I hope you

don't mind, but I made you dinner. Once you said you'd be home, I imagined you'd be tired."

"I'm beat."

"Was the fire awful?"

He leaned against the sink. Was this how life was supposed to be? Exchanging pleasant conversation and coming home to a pot full of happiness and a woman whose smile shone brighter than the sun?

"All fires are awful."

She nodded. "You're right. How silly of me. It was a stupid thing to ask." Before his eyes, the dancing singing girl he'd spied on disappeared and an awkwardness floated like acrid smoke through the air. He had to fix this and fast.

"I like that you asked," he blurted. "All I meant was I've met few fires that weren't awful except for campfires with marshmallows and ghost stories." He moved toward her. "Mind if I taste it?"

Her soft, pink lips lifted into a smile. "That would be great. You can tell me if you want more spices added." Back came the brightness in her voice.

The spoon came out of the pan with a coating of red sauce and a chunk of ground beef cradled in the curve. She lifted it to his lips and waited while he blew on it to cool it down. His mouth wrapped around the edge of the spoon and his taste buds danced in delight as the tomato sauce coated his tongue.

"That's amazing."

She bloomed under his praise. Made him think that she didn't hear positive things often enough.

"I'm so glad. I wanted to make you dinner as a thank you for being so kind to me and the baby."

His eyes dropped to her stomach. "Should you be on your feet?"

Her head bobbed up and down. "Exercise is good. I walked to Main Street today. Doctor Lydia checked my blood pressure, and I met Katie at the bakery who gave me a carrot cake muffin." She bit her lip and stepped back to put the spoon down. "I went to work."

His head tipped sideways. "You went to work?" The woman in front of him was a mystery. Sarah hit four months along and she quit her job. In hindsight, it wasn't because she couldn't work but because she'd started showing.

"Yes, Charlie Whatley gave me a job."

His eyes narrowed. "Should you be working? I mean, you're almost due and your blood pressure isn't the best or is it?" Hope lifted the tone of his voice.

She moved around him to the sink, where she

washed off the spoon. "It's still high, but the job only requires I answer phones and make appointments. Charlie gave me a comfy chair."

His concern was unfounded. She wasn't his to care for. Then again, where were the people that should be caring for her?

"Do you have family nearby?" He moved beside her to twist the cap off his cup and rinse it out.

She took a lot longer than needed to answer that question. It was the kind of pause that made him consider the validity of the answer she'd give him.

"My mother is a phone call away and a few thousand miles. She's in Japan with my stepfather."

That was believable. "What about sisters or brothers or aunts and uncles?"

She turned around and readied the spaghetti for the water that had come to a boil. "My aunt is in Alaska and my grandparents have passed."

She avoided the talk of siblings, which meant she had them and didn't want to talk about them, or she was an only child. He wouldn't press her for details.

"Fair enough. It's too bad you don't have someone to count on who's nearby."

Her shoulders dropped like the air was let out of her. Had he caused that reaction?

"I promise to look for another living situation as soon as I can. On my walk, I saw several vacant properties. Maybe someone would rent to me at a reasonable price."

His heart thumped twice and nosedived into his gut. He hadn't meant to hurt her or to imply she wasn't welcome. He wasn't forcing her to leave. "Oh no. You misunderstood. I'm not looking for you to leave unless you'd feel more comfortable somewhere else. This has to be awkward for you. I'm a stranger."

She smiled, but it didn't light the amber specks in her brown eyes. "You're the nicest stranger I've ever met, and I'll never forget you." She stepped forward and held out her arms like she would hug him and then dropped them and stepped back. Eden Webster was definitely a hugger.

He reached out and tugged her in for a squeeze. "It's going to be okay. This is like summer camp. You never know who your roommates will be. Only, at Camp Cross, the food is better."

Her belly pushed against him. The telltale ripple of the baby moving made his heart warm. He had an opportunity to help her and he would. This was different than before. Eden didn't ask to stay with him. Like him, she was put in a situation that didn't have many options.

This was not his child, but he'd happily help her bring it into the world. It was the right thing to do.

"You've got about ten minutes if you want to shower or change." The puff of air she expelled when she spoke made his uniform flutter in place.

"I think I need a shower."

She inhaled his scent and stepped back. "You smell good. Like a wood fire mixed with sexy cologne." She hopped back another step and turned around, but not before he could see a flush rise to her cheeks.

"I'll be back in a few minutes. I'll set the table and we can eat together if that's okay with you? It's about time I got to know you better, don't you think?"

She nodded but didn't turn around.

He chuckled all the way to the guest bathroom.

The hot water pulsed against his skin like a massage. Fighting fires was arduous work. It didn't matter if he was driving the rig, manning the hose, or humping equipment back and forth from the site, his muscles got a workout.

With his head bowed, he leaned his hands against the cool tile and let the water sluice down his back, washing away the stress of the day. Though he tried to clear his brain, Thomas's thoughts kept going back to Eden. He was dying to know her story, but he wouldn't press her for it. He knew how the wrong story could eviscerate a person.

It struck him as funny that he was willing to help this stranger. Hell, while he hadn't been keen on her coming, now that she was here, he'd let her stay for months if it would help her and the baby. With Sarah, he'd walked out of the hospital ten minutes after Heather was born. He told her he would never raise another man's child. He still felt strongly about that. He'd seen it a thousand times with his friends growing up. His best buddy in high school had to split his time between his father and mother. Blended families were bullshit. The tug of war torturous.

He pushed off the wall and turned off the water. It hadn't occurred to him to get a change of clothes from his room and there was no way he was putting on his soot covered uniform, so he wrapped a towel around his waist. He scooped up his laundry, silently damning James for turning his boxers and T-shirts pink. He tucked the cotton-candy-colored underwear inside his bundle of clothes and strode down the hallway.

When he turned the corner into the master bedroom, he came face to face with Eden.

"Oh, I'm sorry." Her eyes moved over his body like warm honey. Her tongue slipped out to lick her lips. "Let me get out of your way."

They stepped in the same direction. Each time they moved she looked at him like he was dessert. He lowered his roll of dirty clothes in front of his towel to hide his growing arousal.

Get a grip.

"You stay, and I'll move right," she said. She shifted her body and walked toward the door. Before she left, she said, "I hope you don't mind, but I found your laundry in the corner and washed it." She let out a giggle. "I'm assuming you didn't want your undergarments pink."

He had no idea what to say. "You didn't have to do my laundry, Eden."

"I know, but I'm trying to be helpful."

On his dresser sat neatly folded piles of white.

"I don't know what to say."

"Thank you is enough." She moved toward the kitchen, the clack of her soles on the wooden floor muting to nothing.

The homemade dinner was more than he could hope for but turning his underwear white again was pure sorcery. Eden had brought some magic with her presence. What was he going to do with her? Most importantly, what was he going to do with his feelings about her?

His emotions were a tug of war. She was a woman in need of help. No, that wasn't entirely correct. She was a hot woman in need of help. A damn pregnant woman carrying someone else's child and no matter how much his hands wanted to touch her, and his mouth wanted to taste her, she was a problem with a capital P. Pregnancy.

CHAPTER FIFTEEN

EDEN

The phones were steady all day, which didn't give Eden much time to replay the evening in her head. It was downright pleasant from seeing Thomas's near naked body to gorging on pasta and garlic bread. It was a night of overindulgence, but for the first time in weeks, she didn't think about the future. Maybe that was the key to happiness. If she concentrated on one moment at a time, then maybe things would be okay.

"I'm heading home to nurse the boys, but I'll be back at noon when you're off."

"No problem. Take your time." Her eyes lifted to the clock above the desk. It was a cat with a swishing tail, and each time it hit the top of the hour it would meow. At noon it sounded like a cat in heat with its constant mewling.

She did an internet search for adoption agencies. When she pressed the number on her phone to connect, the bile rose up in her throat to nearly choke her. She was halfway to hanging up when a woman's voice answered.

"Providence Adoption Service, how may I help you?"

She opened her mouth several times, but nothing came out.

"Hello?" The voice on the other end was high pitched and chipper. "Hello? Anyone there?"

Eden cleared her throat. "Yes." The one word came out like she was hacking up a fur ball. "I'd like some information, please."

"Certainly. Are you seeking to adopt or looking for loving parents for your child?"

"My child isn't unloved," she snapped.

"I wouldn't dream of assuming that. Often those who come looking for alternatives have found themselves in an unfortunate situation. We can help place your child into a stable family."

"I'm not unstable."

A deep sigh sounded. "I didn't imply that either. Tell you what. How far along are you?"

"I'm due in a few weeks."

"Oh." There was nothing but silence. "Are you looking for compensation?"

"You mean, am I willing to sell my baby?"

"No, we never buy babies. Our objective is to make sure the birth mother is compensated for expenses."

Eden scribbled no on the pad in front of her. "What about the adoptive parents? Are they expected to cough up a fortune to adopt a healthy child?"

"Fees are necessary. Let's start with your name."

"Eden, my name is Eden."

"The mother of all. How perfect." The keyboard tip tapped while she entered Eden's information. "What's the sex of your child?"

"I don't know. Does it matter?"

"Yes, people have a preference and we try to match people's wish list as closely as possible."

"Jeez, this isn't Burger King. No one gets to have it their way. I don't know what sex my baby is. I don't know what his or her ethnicity will be. No idea about height or weight or propensity for disease. I can tell you that this baby kicks like a soccer star and rolls like a gymnast. That's about all I know."

"You have no information?"

"None."

"How about we make an appointment for you to talk to one of our counselors? We can set up testing appointments to get more details."

Her arms came around her belly like an angel's wings to protect and cherish. "You know what, forget it. My baby is not for sale."

She ended the call as Thomas walked in looking hot in his uniform. While he looked great in a towel, there was something about a man in uniform that always got her right in the lady bits.

"You okay?"

She took a deep breath and let out a shaky exhale. "Yes. I'm great."

He stalked forward like a lion on the hunt. "You hungry?" He leaned on the counter and looked at the notepad.

Her eyes followed his to the paper where she'd written the word no at least two dozen times.

"Feeling strongly about something?"

Damn straight she was. She wasn't incubating a designer baby that would go to the highest bidder. She was having a child, and it didn't matter if it was a he or a she. She didn't care if it was destined to be white or ethnic. Blue eyed. Brown eyed. Green eyed. She would love it no matter what. "Wow, I guess I was." She palmed the page and crumpled it up, tossing it into the trash can. "Did you say something about food?"

He reached his hand behind his back and pulled out a box of pure joy. "I got these for you but forgot to give them to you last night."

She took the box of Good & Plenty and held it to her chest. "Where did you get these?"

"You like?"

"Oh, my goodness, I'm like a crack addict with these. It's been days and I'm in withdrawal."

"I bought you a case. You can have them all, or I can distribute them daily to keep the shakes away."

If her heart wasn't already weakened by his full lips, his muscles, and how that white terry cloth towel had hugged the globes of his perfect behind, she'd fall head over ballet slippers in love with the man.

"You're the best. Don't give me the case. I have no control."

"When you get off for the day, I thought maybe you'd like to have lunch at the diner and take a ride with me to see more than Main Street."

It was ten minutes until the clock struck noon, and its inner cat went into heat.

"That sounds like a great plan."

He stepped back and shoved his hands in his pockets.

She tried to imagine Thomas as a teenage boy asking a girl out on a date. She could see him just like he was now but younger, with his hair longer and swept away from his blue eyes. Though this was no date, it was fun to pretend those days hadn't been put to rest for her.

"I'll meet you at Maisey's in about ten minutes."

"It's a date," he said. He shook his head back and forth and rolled his eyes. "You know what I mean."

She pointed to her stomach. "Oh, I get it. Who would want to date this?"

He turned around and moved toward her. "Don't sell yourself short." He rounded the corner and stood in front of her. "You are stunningly beautiful. Your pregnancy takes nothing away from your loveliness."

Had her nipples hardened? Did her thighs clench? Was that an ache in her core or the baby stretching?

"You're hired to boost my ego with regularity."

He lowered to his haunches. "You *are* beautiful. It isn't a line. It's not meant to boost your ego. It's simply the truth." He touched his finger to her nose. "See you in a few minutes. Don't forget to bring your smile." His eyes went to the candy. "And those."

THOMAS WAS SEATED at a table waiting. As soon as she entered, he stood.

When was the last time a man stood up when she approached the table, or opened a door when she entered, or gave up his bed for a stranger?

"Today's special is pot roast and potatoes."

She sat at the chair across from him. "Is that what you're having?"

He rubbed his chin and leaned back as if in thought. "It's a toss between that and a grilled cheese and fries."

"I can see the dilemma." She pulled her napkin from under the silver and set it on her stomach. It appeared more like a bib than a lap covering.

She pulled the menu from the wire rack at the edge. Her eyes moved over the offerings.

"Anything appeal to you?"

Lots of things including one hunky fireman and every kind of pie Maisey had available. "You seem like a sharing kind of guy. I mean, I know you are since you opened your home to me. How about we get one special and a grilled cheese and share?"

God, his smile was like a brand new day.

"I like your style, Eden."

Louise walked over. "Hey, you two." She

159

pulled an order pad from her back pocket. "I'm taking some me time."

"You're working here now?" Thomas asked.

Louise's head bobbed like a broken metronome. "A shift a week until Maisey fills"—she leaned in and whispered, "Meg's spot." She stood straight. "Whatcha gonna have?"

Eden ordered the grilled cheese while Thomas ordered the daily special.

Louise was halfway turned around when she swung back. "Did you get the box of baby clothes I left on the porch?"

Thomas groaned. "She did not because I put them in the garage on my way out, and with the fire I forgot."

Louise tapped him on the head with the pad. "That's okay. I'm sure she has everything she needs but I figured a mother never had too much." She laughed. "Unless it's eight kids." She blew out a whistle. "That last one did me in."

"Eight?" Eden asked.

"Like a staircase, I tell ya. Line them up and you can enter the attic stepping on their heads. Not that we would."

"I'll take care of it when we get home." Thomas looked across the table with downcast eyes. "I'm sorry, it just slipped my mind."

"Anything you can't use you can pass on."

"I can use it all. I don't have anything for the baby."

Thomas and Louise stared at her for an eternity.

"But you're so far along. You haven't been nesting?" Louise cocked her head.

She gnawed at her lower lip. "I've been in survival mode."

Louise's hand settled on her shoulder. "We've got you covered." She spun on her sneakers and disappeared through the swinging doors.

The grip that had tightened around her heart over the last month eased a bit.

Her decision had been building for weeks. That notepad full of the word no was her conscious and subconscious coming together telling her what she already knew. She would never give this baby to a stranger. She would have been happy to give the gift of a child to her sister, but now that her rose-colored glasses had cleared, she realized what a bad decision that would have been.

When she looked up at Thomas, he had a thousand questions in his eyes.

"Tell me about this Meg who only deserves a whisper."

"I'll tell you about Meg, but when I'm through, you and I are going to talk about you."

Suddenly her tongue took on the texture of dry sand. She didn't want to talk about her choices. Said out loud, they made her look like an idiot. She wasn't stupid, just stupidly in love with the idea of having a close relationship with her sister. Stupidly in love with the idea of finally becoming a family. Hell, maybe she *was* stupid.

"Meg worked in the diner for a while," he began. "She was single and looking." He chuckled. "More like single and stalking."

"Did she like you?" Was that pink she saw come to his cheeks? "She did, didn't she?"

"Meg wasn't choosy, she was ... crazy. Fatal Attraction crazy."

She moved in as close as she could to the table. "Like boiling bunnies crazy?"

"Like burn down the Guild Creative Center crazy."

Louise returned with a full tray of drinks and food. "You telling her about our arsonist?"

"Sad that Meg has earned celebrity status."

Louise giggled. "She wasn't a Mae West. More like a female Capone." On that comment, Louise walked toward Doc Parker, who had entered and moved to a corner booth.

"Anyway," Thomas continued. "She wasn't happy that Riley had snagged her man and she set out to destroy the poor woman."

While he spoke, she divided up the plates.

"Sounds like an awful person."

Thomas shrugged. "Who knows why people do what they do?"

"Love. People would do anything for love."

CHAPTER SIXTEEN

THOMAS

"Can you climb up or do you need help?" Thomas held the door of his truck open.

Eden gripped the frame and heave-hoed her body forward but didn't get enough momentum to put her in the seat. "Maybe if I turn around and enter backward." She shimmied her perfect heart shaped ass against the leather and attempted to catch purchase on the running board with her foot.

He could stay there all day and watch her, but it hardly seemed fair to wear her out trying to get in the damn truck.

"I got you." He reached forward and lifted her with ease. "The truck is higher off the ground because of the tires. We get a lot of snow in winter and the extra clearance is good."

"Thank you for that."

He leaned in and buckled her up.

"For what?" Her belt clicked in place and he pulled back.

"For not telling me I was a lard-ass and ate too much."

"You want me to comment on your ass?" He could wax poetic about her ass for hours. She was one of those pregnant women who stayed exactly the same except for their stomachs and possibly their breasts.

"No."

He shut her door and rounded the truck to hop into the driver's seat. "It's perfect, by the way."

She stared out the passenger side window. "What's perfect?"

He started the engine and drove down Main Street. "Your ass."

She shifted her body until she faced him. "Do you have a pregnancy fetish, Mr. Cross? You seem to have a lot of nice words for me."

He stayed silent for a moment. He pulled in front of a big beautiful building with the name The Guild Creative Center etched over the door.

"No, I don't have a pregnancy fetish, although I find pregnant women no less attractive than non-pregnant women. As for my kind words ... I have a feeling you don't get a lot of kind words in your life."

"Oh. I ..."

He slipped out of the truck before she could finish.

Her door opened and he helped her down. The parking lot was uneven, and her shoe caught on a rock, lurching her forward.

Thomas wrapped her in his arms. "Careful now. We don't want you giving birth to a pancake."

When she gained her balance, he didn't let go. He dropped his arms from around her waist. His hand found its way to hers. He'd missed this connection with a person. The simple act of holding hands said more. It implied the two people were connected in a way deeper than the touch. In some ways, that was true with Eden and him. They'd been thrust together by circumstances out of their control.

"This belongs to Samantha and Dalton Black. I thought you might want to see it since it showcases some pretty interesting and varied artistic endeavors."

They walked hand in hand through the front door. He never got tired of walking inside. Loved the smell of creation. On any given day, the air could tell him who was there and who was missing.

He lifted his head and breathed deeply. "What do you smell?"

She followed his lead and breathed in the scents surrounding her.

"I smell something sweet like brownies."

"That would be Dalton and his culinary school. What else?"

She closed her eyes and took in a few more deep breaths.

As she did, he stared at her. He hadn't realized how little she was compared to him. How trusting she had to be to move into his house. He squeezed her hand firmer, hoping to convey that she wasn't alone. He would be there for her.

"Linseed oil." Her eyes fluttered open.

"Yes, that would be Sosie Grant. She normally only comes up from Denver on the weekends."

"Sosie Grant paints here?" Her jaw dropped. "You know her?"

"No, not personally, but I've followed her career because she was this painting savant. She painted a portrait of Christ when she was four that now hangs in the Vatican. She can't be more than thirty now."

"I've only met her once."

167

"She's pretty." Eden walked forward into the gallery where Poppy Bancroft's photos still hung for the world to see.

"I suppose she's pretty if you like tall and skinny. I prefer more curvy women." Without thought, he stepped in front of her and set his hand on her stomach.

They both looked down and then back at each other. "The baby is quiet right now. He always peps up before a meal and sleeps right after."

"He?" Her belly was as tight as a drum. He found his hand moving over it without thought or reason. Only that he liked the feel of it.

"I don't know for sure, but I like that rather than it."

He dropped his hand from her stomach but kept his other fully entwined with hers. "Sorry, I should have asked if I could touch your baby."

This time she turned in front of him and pulled his hand to the rise in her stomach. "You can touch me anytime."

He knew it wasn't an invitation to maul her but something inside him wanted more. His hand moved from her belly to her back and up to cradle her head. In the midst of the display called One Hundred Lifetimes of Love, he lowered his lips to hers. The touch was soft at first.

She gasped and he waited for her to pull away.

Push at his chest. Turn around and march out the door, but she didn't. She opened her lips and let him in.

With his fingers laced with hers in one hand and his other twined in her hair, Thomas kissed her like his entire existence depended on this one kiss.

Soft lips and the taste of black licorice welcomed him. His tongue floated across hers. There was nothing urgent about the moment. This was about seeking and finding comfort in one another.

Her hand fell from his, and he was certain she'd break the rest of their connection, but she didn't. Instead, she raised it to his heart and flattened her palm against his chest. Could she feel it beat at a pace far too quickly and much too hard to be healthy? It damn near thumped out of his chest.

What the hell was he doing? Borrowing trouble for sure. She was pregnant and he knew nothing about her. All he knew was how good she felt in his arms. How wonderful her lips moved against his. How could something that feels so right be so damn wrong?

He stepped away. "I'm sorry."

Her hand flew to her lips. "Me too." She laughed. "Grilled cheese always does that to me."

He loved that she didn't make it awkward.

Hated that she stepped away from him to look at the photos.

"These were taken by Poppy Bancroft, the deputy sheriff's wife." He moved through the larger than life canvases and introduced her to the people of the town.

"What a tribute to her mother." Eden swiped a tear from her eye.

"Are you close to yours?" It wasn't his intention to interrogate her, but the situation opened itself up into finding out more about her.

"Um ... I love my mother, but she moved away nearly a decade ago. We chat on the phone, but I haven't seen her. She met my stepfather after my father died. It's been complicated, but as long as everyone is happy."

"Are you happy?" They said history repeats itself. Poor Eden had her mother move away and since there didn't seem to be anyone knocking down her door over the baby, he could only surmise that the father of her child had abandoned her too.

"I wasn't sure until today, but I am happy. While things are still unsettled in my life, I see the light at the end of the tunnel."

If he thought his heart pounded in his chest at the kiss, it was ready to burst at her confession.

Had that one kiss said something to her that he hadn't been meaning to convey?

"You look like you've seen a ghost." She turned the corner and stared up at a life-sized picture of Samantha Black, who used to be Samantha White, aka Indigo. "Is that Indigo?"

"Slow down a second. Let's go back to are you happy? I shouldn't have kissed you, Eden. I don't want to give you any impression that I'm—"

"You didn't. It was a kiss and it was nice. Thank you for making me realize that my life isn't over because I have a child."

"Why would it be? Lots of women have children on their own."

She lifted her head, and in her eyes, he saw peace. "Yes, but I only decided to keep mine today." She moved away from the picture of Indigo and walked on to a picture of Doc Parker. "Was that really Indigo?"

She was a master of redirection but to ask her to explain would mean he cared more deeply about her than he was willing to admit. "Yes, she's really Samantha Black and this is her building." He pointed past the pictures to a corridor. "Her recording studio is down the hall right next to where Dalton has to be cooking brownies or fudge."

"Wow, that's amazing. I also smell wood or sap."

"The wood would be Cannon, who is Sage's husband." He walked her around the pictures until he found one of Aspen Cove's only bar owner. "The sap could be him or Abby Garrett, who raises bees and makes honey-based soaps and lotions." He moved through the gallery until he found one of Abby in full bee gear in front of a hive.

They left the gallery and walked to the end of one corridor, where a peek through the window showed Riley hard at work on a sculpture.

"Is that a metal piano?"

"Good eye. She's Luke's boss. I mean his girl-friend, but it's the same thing."

"I thought she was a waitress."

"She is. Maisey is her aunt."

They backtracked to the gallery and let their noses lead them to Dalton, who was boxing up what looked like fudge.

"Hey man, have you met Eden?"

Dalton dried his hands on his apron and stepped forward to shake her hand. "Heard about you. Welcome to Black's."

"Nice to meet you," she said in a small voice. "Smells great in here."

Thomas walked around the culinary school. It

wasn't a huge place. There was enough room for four stainless steel work tables, a wall of refrigeration, another full of ovens, and a third that had a prep counter and sinks. Out of the back came Basil Dawson.

"What did you learn to cook today?" asked Thomas.

"Today was death by chocolate day." Basil rushed to get a box and hand it to Eden. "Welcome to Aspen Cove. I'm not a professional, but they won't kill you." He opened the box to show chocolate cookies, fudge, brownies, and a few mini cupcakes.

She reached inside and pulled out a cookie. "Thank you."

He shook his head. "Take the box." He glanced at three others on the shined-to-a-mirror finish table. "I was going to take some to the fire department and police department anyway."

She tucked her cookie back in the box and took it from his hands. "Thomas can take them for you. Everything but my cookie."

"Did you need something or were you giving Eden a tour?" Dalton asked.

"Thought we'd stop by. She hasn't seen much of our town, and since she's staying a while, I figured I'd get her acquainted with what we have to offer."

Dalton lifted a brow that seemed to have a question attached. "Nice of you."

"It's the right thing to do. I'm being neighborly." Thomas hoped that Dalton understood. Then again, he didn't know what his pull to Eden was. Could it be he truly liked her, or was this some sick way his mind was working out his hurts from his past? "Are you ready?" He placed his hand at the small of her back and led her to the truck.

Her phone rang as soon as they exited. She took one glance and frowned.

"Are you going to answer that?"

She shook her head. "Nope."

"Could be someone important."

"They used to be, but now they're not."

Something told Thomas that wasn't anywhere near the truth.

CHAPTER SEVENTEEN

EDEN

Was it Friday already? She straightened her desk and readied herself to leave.

The days passed by so quickly that Eden could barely keep track. It helped that she had a job, her morning check-ins at the clinic, and a man who looked after her. Thomas had been on shift for the last few days, and she hadn't seen him except when he walked her home from work each day.

She found him chivalrous and charming, then again, everything about him was appealing. Her lips could still feel the kiss from several days ago. She could taste him—the sweetness of his mouth as his tongue danced with hers. Feel the strength of his arms around her. Hear his words as he told her she was beautiful. The words were said with such conviction she believed him.

Each day she arrived home, they found something for the baby outside. Today it was a cradle. Hand carved and restored to a pristine finish.

Thomas looked around. "I've never seen this before."

"Who would leave me a cradle?"

He picked it up and carried it into the house like the boxes that showed up each day.

Eden had pushed eight months of giddy joy into several days as she washed and folded hand-me-downs dropped off by anonymous donors.

"Someone who knows the baby will need a place to sleep. It's not like you can put him in a dresser drawer."

She loved the way he'd adopted her habit of calling the baby a he. Each time he stopped by the veterinarian clinic to see her, he'd put his hands on her stomach and ask how he was doing. "He wouldn't know, and he wouldn't complain."

He narrowed his eyes at her. "When he comes out, he's going to protest. Who wouldn't want to live inside your body?"

The way his cheeks heated with a red flush made her giggle.

"You think he wants to live inside me forever?"

He took her coat and hung it up in the closet. "Any smart man would." Knowing he couldn't take back the words, he simply shook his head. "How was your blood pressure today?"

"Better." She pulled her shirt up to show him the belly brace Doc had ordered her. "Look. It's like a bra."

He ran his hands over the elastic band. "Oh good, Sar— I mean I knew someone who had one of those and she found it helpful."

"Who was she?"

He walked into the kitchen and poured her a glass of milk and made her a peanut butter and jelly sandwich like he did each afternoon. It was her new favorite. That and the box of candy-coated black licorice he'd leave for her each morning.

"No one."

Eden knew Thomas carried a huge wound in his heart. He'd slipped several times about a woman named Sarah, but he never offered more than a cursory look into his past. Then again, she'd become a blank canvas too where her life was concerned.

Her phone rang. When she saw her sister's number, she silenced the call. There was nothing Suzanne had to say that she wanted to hear.

"You know, you could block that number."

She licked the jelly from the edge of the bread. "I could, but what if it was an emergency?"

"You wouldn't know because you don't answer the calls." He finished putting everything away and moved toward her. "If it's the baby's father, he has a right to know about his child. Not that it's any of my business, but honesty will always serve you better."

She dropped the uneaten crust of her sandwich to the plate. "This baby has no father."

Thomas chuckled. "Darlin', even I know you can't get that way without a sperm, and the last time I looked, women weren't producing them."

She swallowed the lump in her throat. "You're right, but this baby's father is clueless to his existence."

He scowled at her. When she rose from the chair to put her plate in the sink, he jumped back as if she was a flame and he was tinder.

"What is it with women and honesty? Geezus, Eden, the man has a right to know he's having a baby. You have no right to keep that information from him. I thought you were different, but you're just like Sarah."

"You're wrong. You don't know me. You don't know my situation."

He shook his head. "You're right. I don't know you. You're just a pregnant woman killing time until she has her baby. How selfish are you to keep him away from his father? Does anyone lay claim to this kid? If my memory serves me correctly, you weren't all that sure of keeping him yourself."

She pointed toward the door. "Get out. You stand here and judge me. You act like you know what I'm going through, but you don't. I'm sorry if someone in your life hurt you. It wasn't me. I'm not Sarah. Trust me when I say the sperm that made this baby is clueless. He is because that's the way he wanted it. You act as if I have some devious secret. I don't."

"Not true, Eden. Your phone rings all the time and you silence it. Who's on the other end hoping you'll pick up?"

She fisted her palms. "No one."

"I'm calling bullshit. Each time that damn phone rings, your face pales." He moved toward the front door. "Let me know when you decide to be honest." He swung the door open so hard it dented the drywall behind it. "I'm going to work."

"I'm going to bed."

The door closed behind him, leaving her staring at the dent in the wall. Porkchop moved in and out between her legs. Her meows were like plaintive wails.

It had been days since Eden had cried but the

tears were already spilling down her cheeks. "Damn men."

She bent over and picked up her cat and nuzzled her chin into her fur. "You're so lucky you don't have a man in your life."

Eden moved at a snail's pace to Thomas's room and crawled under his sheets to cry. When the blubbering stopped, she picked up her phone and texted him.

I'm sorry. I have a story to tell if you want to listen to it.

The only one in town who knew about her life was Doc Parker, and to her knowledge he hadn't said a word.

She waited for him to reply but he didn't. Several hours later she woke to the screeching of her cat. Like the mother of a child, Eden flew out of bed and raced to her fur baby. Porkchop was in front of the sliding glass door that led to the back yard. Her fur stood up on end as she clawed at the cat on the other side. A cat dressed in a tuxedo.

She had no one to call. No one who would believe that on the back porch stood a cat in a bowtie and tails. She snapped a picture and stared at it for a long time.

She sent it to Thomas.

Any idea who this is?

He replied a moment later.

That's Tom Brown.

He gave her the name as if the cat was a celebrity in town, and maybe he was. He certainly dressed like one.

She microwaved some macaroni and cheese and climbed back in bed. The house was empty and cold. Not temperature wise but the warmth that came with being friends with Thomas. Had she ruined what they had by keeping her secrets? She wasn't ashamed of the baby. Wasn't ashamed of how he came about. Wasn't ashamed of anything but the fact that she'd believed in her family and trusted they would do right by her, and they didn't. Maybe the most embarrassing fact was a town of strangers treated her better than her sister ever could.

She looked at the dozen or so missed calls from her sister. It was probably time they touched base. She pressed call and waited.

"It's about time."

"Suzanne, I don't want to talk to you. Just tell me why you keep calling."

There was a moment of silence. Eden was certain no one had ever dismissed her sister. She'd always been the pretty one. The successful one. The wealthy one. There was never a lack of praise for her big sister. It was probably why she'd always been so dead set on gaining her favor. If everyone loved Suzanne and she loved Eden, then quite possibly, Eden was worthy too.

"You haven't cashed the check."

Of course, this was about money. It was one of the ways her sister controlled others. She had money and she used it to keep people in line.

"I'm not going to cash the check."

"Don't be an idiot. Having a baby isn't cheap. You'll need it to get out of this situation unscathed."

A heavy weight sat on her chest. "Unscathed? You think growing a human being inside my body for nine months will leave me unscathed? I used to look up to you. Can't believe I wanted to be like you. When you came to me crying that you couldn't have a baby, I gave you one and you tossed it aside like a pair of used Prada shoes."

"Why always so dramatic?"

"I'm not. I'm passionate about the people I love. I love this baby. I'm going to have him and I'm going to keep him. You'll never be a mother, but if you're nice and find some trickle of humanity in your heart, an ounce of love in your soul, I may allow you to be an aunt."

"You can't keep my baby," Suzanne screamed.

"I can and I will." She hung up the phone and turned it silent before she buried her head in the pillow and cried some more.

When the bed dipped beside her, she startled.

"Hey, don't cry." Thomas's voice broke through her sorrow.

When she turned to look at him, he was sitting beside her, a shadow backlit by the hallway light.

"Wh ... what are you doing here?"

He chuckled. "You may have kicked me out, but I actually own the house, so I came back."

She rolled over and buried her face in his lap. "I'm so sorry. I was so wrong. It hurts me to think that you don't like me anymore." Her sobs turned into a choking cry.

"Move over and let me hold you."

She edged back in the bed to make room for him. He lifted the sheets and climbed under with her. There were no words for minutes. He pulled her close to his chest and stroked her hair.

"I want to tell you everything."

He shushed her. "You don't owe me an explanation." His lips brushed the top of her head.

She gripped onto his uniform shirt, her fingers sliding underneath the buttons to touch the soft cotton of his T-shirt.

She took in a shaky breath. "I don't owe you, but I want to tell you if you want to listen."

In the dark room lit by the moon's glow slicing through the slats of the blinds, she opened her heart and soul to a man who had earned her truth.

When she was empty of words, he lowered his mouth to hers and kissed her. It wasn't a kiss of passion or pent-up lust. It was a kiss of understanding and unity. When his lips moved against hers, she knew she wasn't alone.

He rolled her into the cocoon of his arms and cradled her body close to his. "I've got you," he whispered against her mouth. "I've got both of you." His hand splayed protectively over her stomach before she fell asleep.

CHAPTER EIGHTEEN

THOMAS

He woke after the best sleep of his life. Curled against him, her back to his front, his nose buried in her hair was Eden. Her stomach rippled under his palms, the baby stirring awake before her. After an emotional night, he knew she needed her sleep.

Her story floated through his mind. With each new twist in her tale, his heart ached more for the beautiful woman in his arms.

In an attempt to ease the baby back into a quiet state, he slowly caressed her belly. A soothing touch he hoped would lull the child back into slumber.

"You're still here." Her voice was only a whisper.

"I'm not leaving you. Seems to me like that's happened way too often in your life."

She rolled over and faced him, forcing him to shift back to make room. "I'm not your responsibility." She lowered her head until it touched his chest.

"No, but you're my friend, and I like you. I like you a lot. Maybe too much."

"I like you too. Maybe too much." She scooted closer to him. Might have even crawled inside him if there was a path.

He let an arm fold over her, and his fingers pushed into her lower back, where he knew it ached.

"Oh, that feels so good. How did you know?"

He chuckled. "I think one disastrous story is good for now. Let's stick with yours."

She lifted her head to look at him. "Sarah?"

He nodded and pulled her tighter against him. Hell, he'd let her live inside him if he could. Any woman volunteering to have a child for her infertile sister before she had a child of her own was either stupid or a saint. He'd gotten to know Eden while she'd been staying with him. She was far from stupid. The fact that his T-shirts and boxers were white again definitely put her in saint status.

"You hungry?"

"Starved."

"How about I take you to the diner and then we head into Copper Creek? You're about to have a baby and there isn't a diaper in sight. It's time we get prepared for the birth, don't you think?"

"Oh, Thomas, it's all coming at me so fast. I don't know where to begin."

When a sharp kick pressed from his stomach to hers, he laughed. "I'd say let's start with food."

"Do I have time to shower?"

He edged back and placed his hand on her stomach. "Hey, Rocky, you think your mom can have time to shower before she feeds you?"

"Rocky?"

"You've got a prizefighter in there."

"What if I'm having a girl?"

"We'll call her Rockette." He rolled away from her and onto his feet. He couldn't take his eyes off her. Dressed in a T-shirt that fell mid-thigh, she was gorgeous. The glow of motherhood pinked her cheeks or maybe it was because he'd slept with her all night. Could be that he was checking out her legs and those thighs he knew would be lush and comforting.

When he felt the twitch in his pants, he turned and headed toward the door. "I'll meet you in fifteen in the kitchen." He stopped long enough to pull jeans, boxers, and a cotton T-shirt from his drawer before he dashed away.

Living with Eden was agony and ecstasy. She was his biggest nightmare and his greatest dream. Everything he'd longed for and everything he'd lost.

In the shower, as the steam rose around him, he leaned against the cold tile and considered his feelings. How different was she from Sarah?

"Night and day." His voice echoed in the empty bathroom.

Eden's dilemma didn't solve the issue in his mind that she was still having some other man's baby, but even that didn't bother him as much as he would have thought. She had no attachment to the father. No emotional connection. She hadn't been pressed beneath his body calling his name. His contribution was simply one healthy swimmer that managed to impregnate an egg in a petri dish.

Sarah, on the other hand, had lain with her lover one night and the next with him. She'd treated them like menu offerings she couldn't decide between, so she indulged in both. Most aggravating was her boss knew Sarah and Thomas were a couple and Thomas only thought of David Hicken as her employer.

He shampooed his hair and watched as the bubbles turned to clear water when he rinsed. Suddenly like the suds that disappeared, his muddy thoughts washed away.

His problem wasn't with raising another man's child but with raising a child conceived by deceit. It was never about the baby but always about the untrustworthiness of her mother. He'd loved Heather the moment she was born. Hated her mother the moment her lie became his truth.

He turned off the water and stepped into the cool air. Air that surrounded him and invigorated him. He had no idea if what he felt for Eden would go anywhere, but he did know that he'd do everything he could to help her and the baby she carried. If that led to something more, he could honestly say his heart was up for it.

When he walked into the kitchen to find her pouring a cup of coffee into a to-go mug, his insides warmed.

"Yours is fully leaded." She handed him the cup and lifted another. "Mine is not." Her words ended on a sigh. "What I wouldn't do for a Mocha latte double shot with extra whipped cream."

They walked out the front door, only to find another box of baby clothes.

Thomas picked them up and carried them inside.

At his truck, he lifted her into the seat and gave her a quick chaste kiss on the lips. He rather liked them. Liked that their relationship would have to progress slowly since she was weeks away from delivering her baby. There would be no nights of too much alcohol and sex. They'd have to rely on connecting with each other the old-fashioned way—with walks and talks and stolen kisses.

They pulled into a spot in front of the diner. "Do you mind if I run into the clinic for a blood pressure check?"

He raced around the truck to help her out. "Can I come with you?"

Was it possible to light up the world with a smile? Eden's certainly did that for him. He helped her down and threaded his hand through hers.

"I'd like that. I haven't had anyone with me in a long time."

They walked hand in hand into the clinic. Doc Parker was behind the register today.

"Eden, good to see you. Wasn't sure if you'd stop in over the weekend."

"I wasn't sure either."

"Now that you're here, let's see how you're doing." He walked from behind the counter to the small waiting room and into the nearest exam room. "Hop on up."

Doc looked up at Thomas, who stood at the door. "You coming in, son, or you hitting a chair in the hall?" It wasn't a hall any more since Wes Covington, the town's resident builder, did a remodel for his wife, but old habits die hard, and everyone still called it the hallway instead of the waiting room.

"He's coming in." Eden tugged at his hand and pulled him close to her. She backed herself up to the exam table and he helped her onto it. She was a lightweight in his book. Though she'd gained pregnancy weight, he was sure she still weighed little compared to his two-hundred-pound frame.

Standing next to her, hand wrapped around hers, Doc adjusted the cuff and listened as he pumped and let the air loose.

The old man's bushy white brows lifted along with the corners of his lips. "Best I've seen since you arrived." He looked at where Thomas and her hands intertwined. "Must be something agreeing with you."

She looked between the two men. "Yes, my life is sorting itself out. Thank you, Doc. You're the reason I'm here."

Doc looked at Thomas. "I won't be the reason you stay." He rolled up the cuff and set it on the table beside her. "You have a few minutes? I'd like to take a listen to the little bugger's heartbeat. Would you like to hear?" Doc wasn't looking at Eden, his eyes were directed straight to Thomas. If he didn't know better, he'd say that Doc was pulling out all the stops to make Thomas fall for this girl. No one could hear the heartbeat of a child and not melt in awe. "It won't take long. Just a few minutes." Doc walked to a nearby door and pulled an ultrasound machine toward them.

Thomas and Eden exchanged looks.

"What do you say, Eden? You want to hear Rocky?" Thomas asked.

She lay back on the table. "Let's do it. I'm sure Rockette won't mind waiting a few minutes to eat."

Doc took the edge of her shirt and lifted. When he unveiled her bare skin, Thomas flushed. "You want me to step out?"

Doc chuckled. "It's a stomach, Thomas. I'm sure you've seen one before."

He nodded and moved beside Eden. His eyes floated between her face, her stomach, and the screen.

Doc squirted the gel on her belly and rolled the wand over her skin. In seconds the quick *ba bum, ba bum, ba bum* of the baby's heartbeat filled the room.

"Look there." Doc pointed to the screen. "You've got a thumb sucker."

They took in the image on the screen and watched as the baby sucked his thumb. Doc took some measurements.

"You want to know the sex?"

Eden looked up to Thomas.

He cupped her cheek and smiled. "It's up to you, sweetheart." It was the first serious term of endearment he'd used with her.

"I don't think so. Let's keep it a secret. It's kind of like waiting for Christmas morning to see what Santa has put under the tree."

"You heard her. No reveal," Thomas said.

Doc cleaned up her stomach and pushed the machine aside. "I'll see you weekly until you have the baby, which by the latest measurements should be in a couple of weeks. Now go feed that kid before he gnaws off his fist."

Eden hopped off the table. "Can't I pay you, Doc?"

He looked at Thomas and back to her. "You already have."

The next stop was the diner, which was busy today, but a single table remained open and Thomas and Eden slipped into the seats.

Maisey was there with Riley, and a new girl was in training.

"Hey kids." Maisey breezed toward them with the newbie rushing behind her. "This is Natalie. She's a new hire. Just moved here from California. You're going to be her first solo order." Maisey turned on her white loafers and rushed to the window, where orders were stacking up.

"What can I get you?" Natalie asked.

He knew what he wanted. It was his standard breakfast. "Cakes, eggs and bacon."

She wrote down his order. "Juice, milk or coffee?"

He smiled at Eden. "I've had my coffee, how about an orange juice?"

She turned toward Eden. "And for your wife?"

He could see Eden getting ready to correct her, but there was no point. "You want the same, sweetheart?"

She nodded. "No bacon though, I'm watching my salt intake, and I'd like milk please."

Natalie read back the order. "You two are so cute together." She took a glance at Eden's pregnant stomach. "When are you due?"

Thomas smiled. "We're due in a few weeks."

When Natalie walked away, Eden covered his hand with hers. "That was very kind to not point out that you're not the father."

"I wasn't being kind, Eden. You and I are in this together. That's what friends do for friends."

"How was it that I was on my way to Alaska and found myself here?" She squeezed his hand.

He loved the way her fingertips brushed over

his skin like she was memorizing every cell she touched.

"It's the detours that make life exciting." The door opened to the diner and in walked his team. James led the way, with Jacob following and Luke taking up the rear. "Don't look now but here comes trouble."

She turned her head as the three men dressed in their blue uniforms headed their way.

"What is it about firemen? Is there a pre-requisite that says you all have to be model worthy?"

A thread of jealousy weaved through his insides to twist around his gut.

"We made a calendar."

"You did? What month were you?"

"June."

"That's the only month I'd want to see."

How she could coil his insides and iron them with a sentence he didn't know, but she did. "I posed with a Saint Bernard and a gushing fire hydrant."

She fanned her face. "It's getting hot in here."

"You got room for three more?" Luke asked.

Thomas didn't want to share Eden with anyone. He wanted her all to himself, but not sharing her with the world would be like taking every song from every bird or stealing every petal from every bloom. Happiness should be shared.

CHAPTER NINETEEN

EDEN

After breakfast, Thomas took her to Copper Creek. They stopped at a food warehouse, where he picked up another case of Good & Plenty.

"You're going to make me fat."

He wrapped his arm around her shoulder and pulled her into his side. "You're beautiful."

"You're blind."

He pointed to his eyes. "I've got 20/20 vision. I see perfectly."

"Tell me I'm beautiful after I have this baby, and I'm pudgy and soft. What if I get stretch marks?"

"I've got stretch marks. Grew too fast between my sophomore and senior year of high school. They're thin silvery lines that edge up my back.

Kind of look like a growth chart. The only thing missing is the date they appeared." He stopped in the aisle and turned her around to face him. "There is nothing sexier than a woman glowing in pregnancy. Nothing as attractive as one who battles through the birth to produce a life. We all leave this world with war wounds. Some are internal and some are external. No matter what, they are a testament that we lived."

"God, you're something else." She'd never met a man so grounded. "What if your girlfriend gained twenty pounds, would you slap her on the ass and tell her to take it off?" She thought about the time her ex had done that to her, but it was five pounds and was the beginning of the end of their relationship.

"No. While I'd want my girlfriend to be healthy, chastising her for weight gain would never be beneficial. None of us are perfect. It's the imperfections that make us unique. Besides"—he warmed her insides with a smile—"I love a little meat on my woman." He took her hand and led her to the clothing section. "When was the last time you got a new outfit?"

She stared down at her elastic paneled jeans and the oversized T-shirt she wore.

"New? Never. I'm a resale shopper." Her fingers breezed over a salmon colored sundress that hung from the rack. It was pretty in a feminine way. Not something she'd ever buy herself because it wasn't practical. Something she could throw on daily was useful. Wash and wear was better and by the looks of the cotton material, this was an iron before you dressed outfit. She didn't own an iron.

"That would be pretty on you."

Her eyes grew big. "Oh, it's lovely but so impractical."

He picked one off the rack and held it up to her. "Not for what I have in mind." He tossed it in the cart. "Don't argue. Just promise you'll wear it when I take you on a picnic tomorrow."

"Don't you work?"

"Nope. Tomorrow we have a picnic date."

"A date?" She tilted her head and stared up at him. She didn't know what to make of this man. At first, he seemed less than happy to have her in his home. He was never mean, but she could tell that her presence was an inconvenience and how could it not be? Now he was asking her on a date. "Like a real date?"

"You sound surprised." A laugh rolled from deep inside him. "We did sleep together. The least I can do is take you out."

Her cheeks were stand in front of the fire hot,

but the only flame around was Thomas. "We didn't actually sleep together."

He touched her nose with his finger. "Yes, we did. We slept ... together."

They walked down the aisle tossing things in the cart. All along, Eden kept track of the cost of everything. She was close to being at her maximum budget. Thankfully, she didn't need much in the way of baby clothes. She had boxes of them. Everything to dress Rocky or Rockette for the first two years.

When they approached the register with a cart full of diapers and wipes, Good & Plenty, and a beautiful salmon colored dress, Thomas stopped dead in his tracks.

She followed his line of sight to a woman who was equally frozen in place.

"You okay?" She put her hand on his arm. "You look like you've seen a ghost."

He covered her hand with his. "I have. A poltergeist from my past."

The woman he stared at moved her cart ahead in the aisle and began to unload her items.

"You want to talk about it?"

He shook his head as he tossed their items onto the conveyor belt. "No, but we'll have to."

When the cashier told them the total, Thomas insisted on paying.

"I can pay for my things."

He lowered himself so they were eye to eye. "I know you can, and I know you want to, but wearing white boxers loosens the hold on my wallet. You saved me at least this much in embarrassment or replacement costs." He gave her a quick kiss on the lips. "Let me show my appreciation."

She wasn't used to such generosity. First the town and now him. "How did your stuff turn pink?" They moved out of the store and started for his truck.

"James didn't sort the laundry. Up until a few weeks ago, I lived at the fire station. It was James' turn to do the wash. He thought he'd save time and toss it all together."

"Bad move."

"No doubt."

When they got to the truck, he helped Eden inside after insisting he unload the cart. She loved how he took care of her. How he treated her special. Made her feel valued. It was all she ever wanted from her past relationships. Even the one with her sister.

He was rounding the corner of the truck when the woman from the store walked up to him. Her eyes kept glancing past him to Eden. How she wanted to be a fly on the wall of the conversation happening before her.

With Thomas's tense stance, it had to be a doozy.

He turned around to look at her and smiled when he held up one finger. The truck was getting warm, so she opened her door a crack. While she couldn't hear everything being said, she did catch snippets like *you lied, the baby, destroyed me.*

All she could figure was this was the woman who'd broken Thomas's heart. Feeling guilty for listening to a private conversation, she quietly closed her door and hoped they'd finish before she died of heat stroke.

Not willing to listen was different from not wanting to look. She took the woman in all the way from her short dark hair to her denim shorts, perfect for the uncharacteristically warm September day. She wasn't super thin but also not overweight. Pretty was being conservative.

The woman reached into her purse and pulled out a picture, but Thomas turned around and entered the truck.

His hands shook as he started the engine and backed out of the space.

Eden stayed silent, figuring he'd talk when he was ready.

"Are you hungry?"

It had been a few hours since they'd eaten. "I could eat. Are you okay?"

She wanted to reach over and palm his cheek to see if she could stop the tic in his jaw. Soften the hardened muscle. Kiss a smile back on his face.

"I will be. Give me a few minutes. How about a burger? There's a place called Chico's that serves the best burgers in town."

Without knowing the details, she couldn't offer him anything but her company, and if he wanted a burger then she'd be happy to ride along.

"Sounds great." She reached over and set her hand on his thigh. It was an intimate move, but it was important for him to know he wasn't alone.

When his hand moved over hers, she knew he understood her objective.

Minutes later they pulled in the parking lot of a dive called Chico's. It was a walkup with outdoor tables wrapped around the front and side of the building.

Thomas picked one in the shade and told her to trust him when he left her alone to order food. Oddly enough, she did trust him. Enough that she was living with him. Letting him into her doctor's appointments as if he had a say. Inviting him into her heart as if he had earned the right to be there.

When he came back with two red plastic baskets filled with fries and burgers, he sat across from her and let out a long exhale.

"That was Sarah."

Something inside her knew before he said the name.

"I figured."

He took a napkin and folded it in half before he set it between them and squeezed a blob of ketchup in the center.

"She destroyed me."

She stayed quiet and let him talk. It was obviously the day for confessions. It had been less than twenty-four hours since she'd spilled her truths on him, and now he was doing the same.

"She wasn't faithful."

That part broke her heart because Thomas was the kind of man that deserved complete loyalty.

"I'm so sorry."

"She got pregnant and lied to me. Told me it was mine, and I was so excited. Heather was born and ten minutes later her father was banging at the delivery door screaming to see his child."

Her stomach tightened. No wonder he'd looked at her with suspicion in the beginning. Telling her that the father had a right to know. If Sarah had been honest, Thomas would have had choices. Knowing him as she did, the generous man that he appeared to be, made her think if given the choice, he probably would have been there to help Sarah.

"Did she ever apologize?"

He pulled a French fry through the lake of ketchup, swirling it in a circle. "That day at the hospital, I'd cut the umbilical cord and held her." He closed his eyes as if he was reliving the moment. "I had her for ten minutes, and I was in love, then David barged in and said the baby was his." He rubbed his palm over his face. "That's when she apologized. She knew the gig was up. She couldn't lie to both of us at the same time because the lies would be different."

She got up and sat beside him, leaning her head on his shoulder. "I'm so sorry. Did you know him?"

"Not really. He was her boss. I was gone a lot. In a big city fire department, I'd pull lots of shifts. Gone for four days and home for three, sometimes less. When there were fires, we could be gone for days."

Eden wanted to crawl into his lap and hold him. Rock him and tell him it wasn't his fault. "Are you blaming yourself?"

He twisted so he faced her. "I was gone. She was lonely."

She reached up and cupped his face. "Thomas, everyone gets lonely but not everyone cheats. Not everyone lies. Don't let one bad experience dictate your future."

His eyes shifted from hers to her burgeoning belly. As if it was a natural action, his palms melded to the round of her stomach. "I'm so afraid, Eden. So frightened by opening my heart. Scared to death of losing everything again." He swiped at his eye. "You were the worst thing and the best thing that came my way. You opened up a festering wound, but your presence helps heal too."

She wanted to cry for him. "We're friends. That's what friends do for each other."

He moved his hands over her stomach, softly, reverently. "You remind me of everything I lost and everything I want."

She opened her arms and leaned into him for a hug. "I've got you."

CHAPTER TWENTY

EDEN

Dressed in the salmon colored dress Thomas bought her, Eden sat on the couch and attempted to paint her toenails. It was like trying to bend over a barrel and still reach her feet.

He'd left an hour ago to run errands with the promise he'd be back soon and that gave her enough time to pretty herself up.

"I know, baby." She rubbed the top of her tummy where little Rocky was giving her a one-two punch or maybe an undercut for cramping his style. If it was Rockette, she figured the little girl was a gymnast doing a cartwheel with a twist. "Only eight toes to go and Mommy will be finished."

The beat of her heart sped as she said the

word Mommy. Weeks ago, she had been prepping to be an aunt, and now she was a mom. Deep inside, she knew she'd always be a mom but had hoped giving her sister a child would bridge the gap their difference in ages had caused.

A rattle at the front door made her sit back and take a breath. Four toes down and six to go.

Thomas walked in and her already speeding heart ticked up a notch. With his good looks and hard body, he was a dream come true and she couldn't believe her luck. Luck wasn't really the word when it came to Thomas. Doc Parker had everything to do with putting the two of them together. Was it because Thomas's house was the best fit for Eden or was it because Thomas was?

"You look beautiful." He walked inside and closed the door with a push of his hip. Both of his hands were full. One had a large bouquet and the other a paper bag folded and stapled neatly at the top. "Are you hungry?"

Thomas moved like syrup. Everything he did was smooth and with intention. He never appeared to get out of sorts. Always seemed to manage his frustration with a Zen quality.

"I'm starving. What did you get?" She leaned over and tried to finish polishing her toes while he approached.

"I got these for you, though they pale in comparison to your beauty." He offered her the flowers.

"You are the sweetest man. I don't know what to say."

"Say nothing." He took the spot beside her on the sofa. "Show me with a kiss."

She shoved the nail polish brush into the bottle and set it on the table. "Who knew painting my nails would be so hard?"

He stared down at her half-painted toes and laughed. "Kissing me will be easier and far more enjoyable."

Everything he said to her was swoon-worthy. He made her hot and melty when he was around.

She met him in the middle and touched his lips with hers. The hot sear of passion pushed through her like a flame. How in the hell could a man like him want to kiss a woman like her?

Could it be that they were both so broken that the shards left of their lives fit perfectly together? She didn't know, but she didn't want him to stop kissing her.

The feel of his tongue against hers. Strong and passionate. Seeking but not demanding. Offering and not taking. Had she ever been with a person who gave more than they took? She tried to be that person in every relationship. Wasn't it time she took something for herself?

They spent five minutes kissing and when he pulled away, he dropped to his knees before her. "Looks like you can use a hand." He placed one of her feet on his knee and picked up the polish bottle.

"You're going to paint my nails?"

"I am, and then I'm taking you to my favorite spot and we're going to have lunch." With painstaking perfection, he put two coats of polish on her toes.

"You're a pro."

"I've done it before." He helped her to her feet and reached for the sweater she'd thrown over the back of the couch.

"Sarah?" Why did her muscles tense when his ex was mentioned? Could she be jealous? Damn right she was. Sarah had once owned his heart.

"No. My mom broke her hip once, and I polished her nails."

She put on her sandals and lifted her head to stare at him. "I bet your parents are proud of you." She lowered her eyes to look at her stomach. "There's no doubt it's tough being a parent. I only hope that I can raise my child with the integrity and goodness you possess."

"You're going to be a great mother." He picked up the bag of food and moved to the door. "You ready?"

"I'm excited. It's our first date." When he'd put her into bed last night, she wanted to invite him to stay but she didn't want to press. She had no idea where they stood and what this whole thing was about. She'd watched him walk out the room but before the door closed, he told her he was looking forward to their date.

"This thing between you and me is a bit backward."

"I'd say, but I'd be grateful for you no matter how crazy the circumstances."

He led her to the truck and helped her inside.

Mr. Larkin raced over, waving his hands. "Did you get the cradle?"

"That was from you?" Eden asked.

"My mother was rocked in it. I spent time in that thing and so did my daughter and son. No grandkids, so you might as well put it to use."

She slid out of the truck and wrapped her arms around him and hugged as tight as she could. "Thank you so much. It's so special."

"No lead paint. Thought you should know."

Thomas's eyes grew wide. "I hadn't thought about that." He had a look as if he were considering every other surface in the house. "I painted everything but the spare room so no lead there either but we should double check just in case."

She stepped back and leaned on Thomas.

It didn't escape Peter's eyes that Thomas swung an arm protectively around her.

"You kids look good together."

Not wanting anyone to get the wrong idea and force an idea on Thomas, she said, "Oh, we're—"

"On our way to lunch," Thomas finished. He lifted her back into the seat and closed the door. Peter patted Thomas on the back and smiled. The two men talked for a few minutes longer before he walked across the street and Thomas entered the truck.

"What was that about?"

"He was putting dibs on my big screen television in the back room in case I decided to convert it to a nursery."

"That will never happen." She shook her head. "That's your pride and joy. I've seen you talk about that room as if it were a child you were proud of."

She hadn't considered what would happen once she'd had the baby. They were exploring their feelings for each other, but things would change once her child was born. Long-term, Thomas couldn't sleep on his couch while she took up his bed. She'd eventually have to find a place for her and the baby to live. The pace of her heart picked up and the whoosh of blood filled her

ears. She was running out of time to figure it
all out.

Thomas pulled onto the street and drove toward the mountains. "You're quiet."

"Thinking about all I have to figure out, and
how little time I have to do it."

"What's to figure out?"

"You and me. How a baby fits into the mix.
Where I'll live, and how I'll support us when I
have a part-time job. When the baby gets older
who will watch him or her when I go to work?"
She put her hands over her mouth and breathed in
and out.

He took a country road that wound up the
mountain and stopped at the edge of a clearing.
He killed the engine and turned toward her.

"You can stay with me. We'll fix up the spare
room for Rocky and as for you and me, let's move
through that a day at a time. All the world's problems don't need to be solved today. Okay?" He
lifted her chin so she was forced to look at him.

In his eyes, she saw an earnest man doing
what he thought was right. She only hoped it was
right for him as well.

With the bag in his hand, he rounded the truck
and opened her door. "This is my favorite place." He
grabbed a blanket from the truck bed and spread it at

the edge of the overlook and helped her sit. Next, he laid out all the fixings for a picnic lunch down to the juice packs and a box of Good & Plenty.

Looking at the view was like standing on the edge of the earth and seeing it for the first time. In the distance, every color was accounted for. The last of the aspens for which the town was named were turning gold. The forest was blazing with orange and red and yellow. The evergreens acted as the backdrop to the explosion of fall around them.

"Turn around and look at me."

When she did, he snapped a picture of her with nature's landscape in the background.

"Beautiful."

She looked over her shoulder at the canyon. "It is. Thank you for sharing it with me."

"I was talking about you." He turned the camera to show her the photo.

She hardly recognized herself. She was as big as a hippo, but there was a serene look in her eyes. If she didn't know better, she'd say the woman in the picture was telling her everything would work out fine.

"Let's eat." She opened the box of fried chicken and served them both. Thomas had thought of everything from wet wipes to a citronella candle that made the moment romantic and also kept the mosquitos from biting.

After the meal was finished, they stood at the edge looking out at the world. From this perspective, anything was possible. He moved behind her and wrapped his hands around her stomach before nuzzling into her neck.

"You're breaking down the steel walls of my heart, Eden."

She turned to face him. "Your heart is too big to encase, Thomas. Let it out. I promise to protect it." She lifted on tiptoes to kiss him. "Your heart is safe with me." This was the kind of man she'd dreamed about. "I have no idea where this will go, but for right now, it's perfect."

She laid her head against his chest and listened to his heartbeat. After several minutes, hers beat in rhythm with his.

"Shall we go home?"

She liked the sound of that. "Will you sleep in your bed tonight?"

"Only if you're there with me."

"I'll be there." She giggled. "I take up more than half, but I'd like you next to me if that's not too weird."

"Not weird at all. Beside you is where I want to be."

They packed up the leftovers and blanket and

headed back home. After a night of canoodling on the couch watching sitcoms, they went to bed.

She turned on her side and Thomas tucked a spare pillow under her stomach. He was always so attentive to her needs.

He spooned behind her with his palm splayed over her belly. Before she fell asleep, she heard him say, "If all of this went away, I'd never survive."

CHAPTER TWENTY-ONE

THOMAS

It had been two weeks since Eden had invited him into her bed. Each night he was able he molded himself to her and fell asleep breathing her scent. She used the same shampoo as him, but she always smelled like a sweet confection. The carrot cake muffins used to be his favorite. The aroma always floated down the street to the station, but they had nothing on Eden.

His eyes shifted to his phone at least a dozen times each morning he pulled his shift. Her texts invigorated him for the day.

While he loved his job, he hated the shifts that pulled him from the bed. Each night he'd sneak back home and watch her sleep. Before he left, he placed a box of her favorite candy on the night-stand along with a note.

"You got it bad." James flashed past him, grabbing the phone from his hand.

"Return it or die." Thomas was beginning to think that there should be an older age requirement for firefighters. The younger guys were still wet behind their ears and the high school antics they played grated on his nerves.

Last night he'd climbed into his bunk to find his bed short sheeted. Last week Jacob switched the sugar for salt. He claimed it was an accident, but Thomas knew better.

"Incoming text," James yelled as he fled the crew kitchen and took off toward the rig.

"James," he warned. "If I don't get that phone back in less than five seconds, I'll make sure you pull every Saturday until you turn old and gray." James hated the Saturday clean up. The day they spent hours shining up the station and the vehicles. Since Thomas was the scheduler, he could do it.

"She says she misses you." He moved from the backside of the rig and handed him the phone.

Thomas sat on the bumper and watched the dots move as Eden typed more.

I miss you. So glad your last night-shift is over. Thank you for the candy

and the note. You were a nice surprise too. I'll be leaving in a few minutes for my shift. Can you do lunch?

He knew his grin was big because his cheeks ached from it. Last night he'd written a heartfelt note that said his life changed when she entered it. She was a nice surprise. He wasn't looking for anything but something special managed to find him. He always ended his notes wishing her and the baby a beautiful day.

"When are you going to marry her?" James plopped down on the bumper next to him.

"We're friends. You don't marry someone who's only a friend."

James lifted his brows. Brows Thomas knew without a doubt he got groomed regularly by Marina. They were far too perfect to grow that way naturally.

"For being an old man you're an idiot." James slid a few feet away, no doubt gaining distance in case Thomas decided to retaliate.

"I'm older, wiser, and all-around superior to you. You with your cotton candy dreams. Wait until some woman reaches into your chest and rips out your heart. You'll wise up about relationships mighty fast."

"Even I know you marry your best friend." He pushed off the truck and started for the kitchen.

"You and Jacob will make a handsome couple."

James flipped him off before he entered the kitchen.

Thomas glanced back at his phone. There was nothing else there.

He moved to the office where Luke sat behind the desk reading the latest Jack Reacher novel.

"Would you say you and Riley are best friends?" He shouldered the doorjamb.

Luke earmarked his page which would have sent Thomas's mother into a tailspin given she was a librarian and books were equivalent to gold.

"What do you mean?" Luke tossed the book on top of the desk.

"Do you think your fiancée or spouse should be your best friend?"

Luke rubbed his chin and stared at the ceiling. "There's room for more than one best friend." He kicked his feet off the desk and leaned forward, resting his elbows on the hard wood surface. "You're my best friend, but I refuse to sleep with you. There are things I tell Riley that I'd never tell you. Personal things."

Thomas shook his head. "Yeah, I don't want to know when you get an ingrown hair on the underside of your sack."

Luke stared at him with a neutral expression. "I'm a waxer."

"Shit. Really? I didn't need to know that." He rubbed his eyes, but his imagination was vivid.

"See? Things your woman would know but your friends probably shouldn't. It was a joke anyway. No one, and I repeat no one is moving toward me with hot wax."

A whoosh of air left Thomas's lungs. He experienced the process as he considered it. The oozing of hot wax and the inevitable ripping off of hair. His own sack crawled inside his body at the thought.

"Is this about Eden?"

He pushed off the doorframe and took a seat in the chair across from Luke.

"I guess." Where did he begin to explain when he couldn't make sense of things himself? "She's got me all twisted up inside, man. I don't know if I'm coming or going."

"You like her. That's a good thing."

"I do, but shit ... she's pregnant with another person's child." Eden had come clean to several people about her situation and news had spread like a grass fire.

"So. Do you like her enough to get past that?"

Thomas inhaled so deeply he was certain his

lungs would pop. "Here's the thing ..." He reminded Luke of the situation with Sarah.

"It's not the same. You know that, right?"

"I know, but it feels the same on many levels and I keep beating myself up because I left Sarah and the baby I'd always considered mine even when she begged me to stay. I promised myself that I'd never raise another man's child."

Luke sat for several minutes in silence. When he spoke, he did so in a somber, here's-my-take fashion. It reminded Thomas of the way his father dealt with everything. Had Thomas acted with his heart or his head when it came to Sarah? Seeing her a couple of weeks ago raised all of those emotions to the surface again.

The love.

The loss.

The lies.

"Do you love Eden?" Luke asked.

He knew the answer immediately, but he held back the yes. "What does love have to do with it?"

Luke chuckled. "Everything. There are things you'd do for love that you would never do otherwise."

"Like raise another man's child?"

"I guess, but in the end, the child is Eden's, and in the case of this child, it's whoever's going to love it best. DNA doesn't make you a daddy.

What's the hang-up? I don't think it's about the baby not coming from you. It's deeper than that."

"Now you're a therapist?" He crossed his arms over his chest. Analyzing the situation had become a favorite pastime. He had years to come up with the conclusion he knew Luke would find in moments.

"I'll send you a bill after we're done."

"Fine," he grumbled. "What's the diagnosis, Doc Mosier?"

"You're afraid."

A *pfft* sound blew past his lips. The air that whizzed out strong enough to send a paper from the inbox fluttering to the floor.

"Fear isn't my problem. Falling for the wrong woman is."

Luke bent over to pick up the paper. "Fear is your problem. You're afraid what happened last time will happen again. You open your heart and fall in love and something is going to strip you of all that joy again."

"It's possible."

"It's exactly what's happening but this isn't the same. There's no betrayal. There's no man on the sidelines who doesn't know he's having a baby. Eden was honest with you. That is where the difference becomes apparent. You can lie to yourself as to why you didn't stay with Sarah, but it wasn't because the baby wasn't yours. It was because she lied to you. She handed you the Kool-Aid and you drank it. Deep inside you knew if you stayed with her, you'd never be able to trust her. Eden isn't Sarah. She came clean once she knew you well enough to trust you."

There are things you tell someone you love that you wouldn't tell anyone else. Eden had trusted him with her secret. A secret she kept not because she was being dishonest with anyone but because she was embarrassed for herself. Ashamed that she'd trusted another. In some odd ridiculous way, she'd experienced the same kind of betrayal. Only hers was far worse.

Thinking about what her sister and brother-in-law did to her made Thomas want to go postal, but he was a thinker more than an emotional reactor, much like his father. It was only in moments of deep despair that his heart ruled over his head.

"I love her. Can't help it. She's the best person I know." He said the words aloud despite them starting as an internalization. They tasted sweet on his tongue, much like Eden's kisses. Funny how the truth had a different flavor than a lie.

Luke slapped the desk. "My job is finished." He looked at his phone. "I think you owe me lunch."

"I've got a lunch date with my girlfriend." The

word rolled off his tongue like a song. Everything about Eden and his feelings for her was right and rang true in his heart. "I'm out of here." He stood and walked toward the door. "Thanks for being my best friend."

Luke followed him. "No problem, man. Just don't tell me anything that I can't erase from my brain."

Thomas grabbed his jacket and jogged to the vet clinic. He couldn't get to Eden fast enough. There were words that needed to be said.

He opened the door to find her sitting on her chair, her eyes opened wide and her cheeks flushed.

She held up a hand. "Don't come any closer. I don't want you to see me."

He twisted his head. "Sweetheart. I see you anyway."

"No, not like this."

He couldn't quite figure it out. Did she accidentally put on mismatched socks or shoes?

"You know I'll love you no matter what." The words were out but she hadn't noticed. Hadn't heard them.

"Oh God, not again." She disappeared, bending over so he couldn't see her above the desk.

"What's wrong?"

She lifted her head and tears rolled down her cheeks. "I don't want to tell you."

His heart stuttered. Was this where his dreams died?

"Eden." He moved toward her. "Whatever it is, we can get through it."

Her shaky inhale came out the same. Jagged and harsh.

"You promise you won't feel weird."

He had no idea what he'd feel but it had to be better than the pure fear he was experiencing now. A clawing gnawing terror he had to hide so she didn't feed into it. "Nothing you tell me will change the way I feel about you."

"My back hurts. I got up to walk the tension out and ..." She looked down. "I wet myself. I'm a sopping wet mess and I smell bad."

He wanted to laugh. He pulled in his next breath and smiled. The scent of ammonia floated through the air. He moved around the desk to kneel in front of her. "You didn't wet yourself, baby. Your water broke." He leaned in and kissed her. It was a tender, loving kiss. One he hoped conveyed everything he was feeling inside. "We're going to have a baby."

CHAPTER TWENTY-TWO

EDEN

Palm to her forehead. Of course, that was the problem. The issue was she hadn't experienced any pain. A dull nagging ache in her lower back and a gush of water that never seemed to end.

"Oh, my God, I'm not ready."

"Yes, you are. It's going to be okay." He stared down at the puddle. "Let me mop this up, and I'll get you to Doc's clinic so you don't give birth here in the veterinarian clinic."

Her heart warmed to watch him jump into action. He grabbed the mop and bucket Charlie kept at the ready for what she called piddlers. Never in her life had Eden considered she'd be one.

"Are you in pain at all?" He offered her his hand and pulled her to a standing position.

"There's a tightness in my stomach. A horrible ache at my back, but nothing I can't bear. Surely, having a baby is going to hurt worse than this." She wasn't trying to borrow trouble, but everything thus far was bearable except for the embarrassment of letting Thomas see her.

"Let me carry you?" He bent down and attempted to scoop her behind the knees, but she scrambled back, nearly slipping on the damp tile.

"No way, you'd be soaked. I'm like a leaky faucet."

"Can you walk?"

"Yes, I can walk." She maneuvered around him and took several steps toward the door when the first pain hit her with the force of a head-on collision. "Oh, holy hell." She doubled over and held her stomach, panting until the pain passed.

She scurried out the door before another could hit. Once it was locked, she moved with haste down the sidewalk, Thomas rushing behind her. In front of the window of the diner, the next pain hit hard and nearly sent her to her knees. She found herself whisked into his arms and heading at a near run toward the clinic.

He pushed through the door and told Agatha, who was behind the counter, that the baby was coming and coming fast. Being a Thursday, it wasn't a clinic day.

Eden experienced a moment of panic when she considered Doc might not be around. She knew Lydia was out of town because she'd popped in this morning and told her to not have the baby today because she was visiting friends in Denver.

"Is Doc here?" she called over Thomas's shoulder while he rushed her into the exam room.

"I'm here." His footsteps moved down the stairs at a faster clip that she would have expected from a man his age. "Hey, Lovey. Get Sage down here to help."

"Right away."

"Shouldn't I go to the hospital?"

Doc was a whirlwind of activity, pulling out instruments and lab coats. He tossed a set of scrubs to Thomas and told him to change.

He laid her on the exam table and kissed her. "I'll be right back."

As soon as he left, another slicing pain ripped through her. "Oh God, it's a wonder women have more children after the first." She puffed air through her mouth the way she'd learned in the few classes she'd taken before the move.

"I'm assuming you want Thomas in here with you." He lifted his ready to take flight brows. She focused on them rather than the pain. The white hair swept up like dove's wings on each side. "If not, I can ask him to stay in the waiting room."

She puffed through the pain. When it ebbed, she answered. "No, I need him here."

Doc smiled. "I thought so. He's a good man, Eden."

"He's the best."

"Let's get you undressed and in a gown while we can." Doc helped her down. She shrugged off the sodden pants and stripped out of her clothes before pulling on the hospital gown. This was not the time for modesty.

The door opened and in rushed Sage. "I hear we're having a baby?"

"Yes," Eden got out before the next surge rushed through her and another gush of water hit the floor. "Jeez, how much amniotic fluid could there be?" No sooner were the words out before Thomas raced in dressed in green scrubs. The man looked great in everything. Hell, she was certain he looked great in nothing, although she couldn't vouch for that from personal experience. Each night they climbed into bed, he wore shorts and a T-shirt.

She bent over and palmed her knees as another pain approached.

Sage moved around as if preparing for afternoon tea. She wasn't harried or concerned. Eden remembered learning Sage was a trained labor and delivery nurse. There was nothing that seemed to fluster her. Even if she'd walked in with the baby hanging between her knees, she was fairly certain Sage would have looked at her and with a calm reserved for much older people would have said, "Oh, let's go have a baby."

Doc patted the table as soon as the worst was over, and Thomas helped her up. The way he looked at her was the same way a kid looked at a wrapped gift. Having the baby would be exactly like that. Everything about him or her was a surprise.

Thomas pressed his lips to her ear. "I'm here. You're beautiful, Eden. So damn beautiful."

"You're a blind man, and I love it." She wanted to tell him she loved him, but she couldn't just yet. She needed to be certain what they were feeling wasn't simply the euphoria of sharing the experience of bringing a child into the world.

Once it was all said and done and midnight feedings and dirty diapers became a regular occurrence, would the magic of what they shared be gone?

Doc and Sage stood at the end of the table. "Let's see where we're at."

Doc did the exam while Sage looked on and wrote in Eden's medical record.

"How long have you been feeling these pains?"

"The pains only began just after my water broke but my back has been aching since last night. I figured it was the muscle thing I had the last time." She gritted her teeth and blew puffs of air through her open mouth. "Son of a biscuit," she yelled.

Thomas held her hand while she squeezed.

"You've got quite the grip."

She turned to him. "Did I hurt you? I'm sorry. It's just ..."

Doc pulled the sheet over her legs. "There's good and bad news," he said with a smile. "Bad news is you aren't going to make it to the hospital if that's where you wanted to have your baby. I could call an ambulance, but you'd probably have the little one on the way."

"And the good news?" Thomas asked.

"You're going to be one of those women made for having babies. Short, hard labor, but I'd bet in less than an hour you're going to be a mom."

She didn't have time to react because another contraction seized her. Thomas moved his head so his chin rested on her shoulder and his lips were near her ear. "Let's breathe through it, sweetheart. We'll do this together."

That's how the next forty minutes went.

Thomas helped her breathe through every pain. He held her hand but never complained when she nearly broke his fingers. When it came time to push, he lifted her up, supporting her back while she bore down.

"Almost, Eden," Sage said. "Another two pushes and you can meet your baby."

Doc looked at both of them. "Up to you, Eden, but where do you want Thomas?"

"With me all the way. We're a team."

"I can see that, but my question is, do you want him to help deliver your child? I know he's done it before. Could make it special for the two of you."

She looked up at him. Was that hope in his eyes? Did he want to help deliver the baby? She flagged him closer. Her words were only for him. "Do you want to deliver the baby?"

He smiled at her. His eyes full of love and emotion. "I'd love to deliver our baby."

Her heart hitched in her chest. The squeeze was so hard it took her breath away.

"I never imagined the first time you'd see me naked it would be like this."

"But I should stay here and be with you. Let's experience this together." He pressed a kiss to her lips. "I've told you before. You are the most beautiful woman I know. You were yesterday. You are today, and you will be tomorrow."

The next pain built. It crawled down her spine to twist her core.

He never let go of her. His lips were a whisper in her ear. "You've got this, baby. One more good push."

"Yes, let's make this a good one," Sage whispered. She stood back and prepared for the handoff.

Eden pushed to the count of ten while Thomas supported her back.

"Oh, sweetheart. The baby has a full head of hair." His voice was full of wonder.

The next contraction came like a lightning bolt. "This is it, Eden," Sage coached. "Give us a big push."

She sucked in a breath and counted in her head. One. Two. Three. Four. On number five the pressure was gone, and the wail of her baby moved through the room.

She let out a sigh of relief.

"You have a perfect baby boy," Doc said.

She lifted on her elbows to see him.

Doc wiped what looked like cold cream from his skin and laid him on her chest. His crying stopped immediately. It was as if he sensed her and knew he was safe and at home. His ear pressed against her breasts while his tiny mouth rooted around.

"Can I cut the cord?" Thomas asked.

She looked at him and saw the tears in his eyes. This was an emotional moment for him. She saw him glance at the door as if expecting a man to rush in and claim the baby, but Eden knew that would never happen.

"Yes, Thomas. Cut the cord and make him ours." It seemed to her that while the baby was attached to her, he'd be hers, but the minute the tie was severed he'd become theirs. No matter what happened in the future, whether Thomas remained in her life as a friend or maybe more, this moment would be important because without him, she'd be lost. He was her lifeline. Her thread to safety. Her connection to happiness. Thomas would always own her heart.

"Do you have a name for the baby?" Sage took him and cleaned him up. She weighed him and swaddled him and handed him back to Eden.

She looked at Thomas and then at Doc Parker. "His name is Thomas Parker."

"That's a mighty fine name," Doc said. "Sage tells me you're breastfeeding, so let's get Thomas to take the teat."

When Eden looked at Thomas, the big burly man beside her, she saw him blush.

Sage showed her how to get the baby to latch on and once he did, she walked to the door. "I'm going to give you a few minutes to get acquainted." She turned and walked out, leaving them alone.

"You named him after me?"

With one hand cradling the baby, she reached up to cup his cheek. "I can't think of another man who is more worthy than you. If he grows up with a tenth of your kindness and compassion, he'll be a better man than most."

"Eden, I love you."

She smiled. "I love you, too."

The words were out. They were everything she wanted to hear and feel and say.

He looked down at the baby nursing.

"I'm a bit jealous." He cupped baby Thomas's head. "I've been obsessed with your breasts from the first day I met you and never have my lips been on them."

"I'll feed you later," she said.

"Promise?"

"I never lie."

There was more to that declaration than a promise to let him suckle her breasts. She knew, and by the smile that softened his face, he knew it too.

CHAPTER TWENTY-THREE

THOMAS

Three blissful weeks had passed, and loving Eden and the baby had become first nature to Thomas because second nature was too far removed.

He sat on the edge of the bed and stared at how beautiful she was. Her hair curtained her face. Her lips looked so damn full and kissable. It was the only thing they'd done, but a day without a kiss from Eden was like a lifetime without sunshine.

Clearly feeling his presence, she stirred and opened her eyes.

"Good morning." With a sweep of her hand, she brushed the remaining hair from her face.

"Morning beautiful." He cradled Tommy in his arms. They'd decided to shorten the name to avoid confusion. Looking at the boy, it was hard to imagine anyone not wanting him; then again, Eden's sister hadn't had the honor of staring perfection in the face. Now he had both Eden and Tommy.

She lifted her hand to play with his tiny toes. "Look at you two. I'm the luckiest woman alive."

God, her smile was captivating. He'd never tire of it.

"Nope, Tommy and I are smitten with Mommy."

She set her hand on his thigh and stared up at him with eyes that no doubt held love and gratitude. Misplaced thankfulness that traveled in the wrong direction.

A couple of months ago, he was content to sit in the house and watch a big screen TV while life moved forward at a pace far too fast to comprehend.

"Did he eat?"

"I fed him, burped him and changed him. He's happy."

After a week of every two-hour feedings, Eden had started pumping her milk so he could help.

He told her it was a wise move so she could sleep and that was part of it, but his motives were selfish. He loved sitting in the rocking chair that had magically shown up on his porch the day after

Tommy was born. He'd cradle the baby in his arms while Tommy stared up at him. Those eyes of his were mesmerizing.

"Do you have to work today?"

"I do, but I'll stop in when I can."

Wouldn't it be great to be independently wealthy? He couldn't complain; he had enough money to live comfortably. Enough to provide a comfortable life for Eden and Tommy. All he needed to do was convince them both that life with him was worth it.

She shimmied up to lean against the headboard. Her oversized nightgown hung off her shoulders to reveal the fullness of her breasts. Breasts he'd seen a thousand times in the last few weeks and not once had touched but desperately wanted to.

"Tommy and I are going to work too."

Porkchop hopped on the bed and sauntered on the fringe. She wasn't certain how this wiggly little boy fit into the mix, but both he and Eden made sure to give her extra pets each day to make sure she didn't feel neglected.

"You know I'm happy to take care of you both."

She lifted her hand to cup his cheek. "You're a good man, Thomas. A saint really, but I need to take care of myself too. It was my decision to have this baby all the way from the beginning, and it doesn't matter if I took a detour. I'm more than happy to go to work." She giggled. "I can't really call it work since all I do is ogle Tommy and answer the phones."

"Pretty sweet job." He understood her need to be independent. She'd just been taught that people can't be trusted. Her sister should have been the one Eden could depend on, but she'd turned her back on her. "You talk to your mom?"

"She's over the moon. Expects me to send her a picture each day so she can see how much he grows."

He hated to ask, but there was always a fear that her sister would change her mind. "Any word from Suzanne and Brady?" Funny how he was on a first name basis with them but how could he not be? They'd put the woman he loved in a bad situation. She willingly and without pay rented out her womb for the love she craved, the family she so badly wanted, and they abandoned her when she was at her most vulnerable. When she was homeless, next to broke, and eight months pregnant.

"No, then again, I blocked her number, but Mom hasn't said anything about her." Her eyes fell at the same time as her smile. "She's really missing out." Eden shrugged. "Wouldn't matter at this point. I'd never give him up."

He was happy to hear that because some part of him thought if Suzanne came back and demanded the baby, Eden would do what she thought was right. Somewhere in her beautiful, kind mind, she'd justify that Tommy would never be here if it wasn't for Suzanne and her fleeting desire to be a mom.

"I'll never give either of you up." He leaned in and gave her a kiss. "You want to shower?"

Her brows lifted. "Together?"

He chuckled. "Don't tease me. I'm a mere mortal."

"Hard to believe."

He looked down at his growing erection and shook his head. "I'll make coffee. Tommy and I will be in the kitchen waiting for you."

She slid off the bed, her T-shirt skimming the tops of her thighs. How she, in the course of three weeks, had slimmed down to her current size he didn't know. Eden pregnant was a turn on. Eden not pregnant was a damn wet dream. One he was certain he experienced nightly tucked up next to her body.

She complained about her soft stomach and wide hips, but all he saw was perfection.

Fifteen minutes later, dressed in jeans and an off-the-shoulder sweater, she walked into the kitchen smelling of cotton candy.

"Decaf the way you like it with a half a cow's daily production of cream and two scoops of sugar."

"Hey, I have to have some kind of vice. I gave up my daily box of candies."

"You didn't have to. I liked being able to put that smile on your face."

She sipped her coffee then looked over her shoulder at her bottom.

"Have you seen my ass?"

Wrong thing to ask him. "Yes, and it's perfect." He'd seen it. Copped a feel at night when they were spooned together. Fantasized about the moment when her flesh would fill his palms.

"You need an eye exam."

He glanced over at Tommy, who was asleep in his carrier. It was perfect timing to bask in the warm glow of her sunny kisses. He moved both of their bodies until she was pinned against the kitchen counter. "I see you. Always have. Always will. Now kiss me so I can have the taste of you on my lips for the rest of the day."

He gripped her hips and lifted her. Normally he'd set her on the counter and practically kiss her face off but today he shifted away from the granite, which forced her to either hang like a rag doll in his hands or wrap her legs around his waist.

"I'm going to wrinkle your uniform."

"I don't care. All I care about is this moment, wrinkles be damned." He pressed his mouth to hers and everything else evaporated. He wanted so much more, but this was enough for now.

Their kisses were the equivalent of making love. Nothing innocent about the way she let him in. The way she coaxed his heart to open. The way his whole body responded to the touch and taste of her. Months ago, he wouldn't have believed a kiss could change everything about his life, but Eden had. She'd brought him hope and love and Tommy.

A sharp rap on the door separated them. The sound was so loud Tommy startled, throwing his arms to the side. His eyes shot open wide and his lips quivered before he split the air with a cry.

"I'll get him, you go see who's pounding down the door," Eden said.

Thomas left them in the kitchen and stalked toward the door ready to do battle. Everyone in town knew they had a newborn. Besides, it wasn't even eight in the morning. Polite visitors called after nine. At least in Aspen Cove they did. Most people were like ninjas and spirited away after leaving tokens of their support on the porch. Not a day went by where a package of diapers, or wipes, or a basket of fresh muffins didn't arrive. That was the beauty of the town and its people. They didn't need to be seen to be valued. No words were expected. The gifts came from a different place. They came from the heart. A bold statement that said you are part of a community. He was so grateful to have found this little slice of heaven in the mountains of Colorado.

When he flung the door open, he didn't face anyone he knew. Somewhere deep inside a feeling of dread bubbled inside him. Maybe it was the suit. The crazy tie that said, "I'm an asshole," in bright red. This was a man that wanted to be noticed, and he wasn't delivering diapers.

"Can I help you?" Thomas hardly recognized the tone of his voice. It was deep and imposing. He hoped it conveyed a don't mess with me vibe.

"I'm looking for an Eden Webster. I'm told she is residing here."

Thomas glanced behind him to watch Eden inch toward the door with Tommy cradled in her arms.

As much as Thomas wanted to protect her, to stand in the doorway and not let this man even glance at what had become irrevocably his, he knew she'd heard him mention her name.

"I'm Eden." Just a whisper moved past her lips. She inched into the small space beside him. Looking at the baby and back at him, she lifted Tommy into Thomas's arms. "Can I help you?"

The smarmy man smiled as he pulled an envelope from his pocket. "You've been served."

He spun on his wingtips and strode down the walkway.

Thomas stood in the doorway with Tommy held close to his chest. He stayed there until the man climbed into his sedan and disappeared.

It wasn't until a gasp from Eden pulled his attention back.

"She wants the baby back."

If he hadn't been holding on to Tommy, Thomas would have collapsed to his knees. This was the way of his life. Get a taste of something wonderful only to have it ripped out of his grasp.

He marched over to Eden and somehow managed to hug her while holding the baby. "Not gonna happen, sweetheart. I just got you, and I'm not ready to give either of you up."

He made a silent pledge right there that this time he'd fight to the death for Eden and their baby.

CHAPTER TWENTY-FOUR

EDEN

Eden stumbled to the couch and collapsed.

"They want the baby. They are taking me to court to get him back." She was too upset to produce the tears she wanted to shed.

Thomas took a seat beside her, all the while cradling Tommy in his arms. This was where the baby belonged. He needed a man like Thomas to raise him. A man who would cherish him and appreciate him for everything he would be and wouldn't be. She knew that Thomas would guide their boy to be a man like him and if he wanted to weave baskets for a living, he'd support that as much as a career in public service.

"Did you tell her you had the baby?"

She shook her head. "No, we haven't spoken. I blocked her number, remember?"

He ran his palm over Tommy's hair and smoothed it down. Despite all the commotion, he'd fallen asleep because he felt safe and secure and cared for.

"She knew your due date so she would assume you had him. Maybe she's feeling deserter's remorse."

Eden hopped off the couch and raced to the kitchen for her phone. "No. She's been talking to my mother." She dialed her mom's number. Didn't care what time it was in Japan.

When her mother answered, she cried, "How could you?" She put her on speaker so she wouldn't have to repeat everything for Thomas.

"Eden, what's wrong?"

"You told Suzanne I had the baby."

"Well, of course I did. She's an aunt. She should know."

Thomas groaned. "It's more complicated than that," he said aloud. "She's now suing Eden for custody."

Silence filled the room. "Oh, honey, I'm sorry."

"You sent her a picture, didn't you?"

Her non-response was the answer. "He's such a beautiful child."

"He's my child, Mom. She doesn't get to return him and then ask for him back."

"Now, honey, it's a complicated situation. You wouldn't have him if not for Suzanne."

She knew it was true, but it didn't matter. If she'd followed through with what Suzanne had asked of her, the baby would be in someone else's care and the likelihood of getting him back would be nil.

"No, Mom, he wouldn't be here if not for me. I'm fighting to keep him. I'm not asking you to choose sides, but dammit, why does she always get what she wants?"

Her mother sighed. "Because your sister never understood the word no."

She shook from her toes to her head. "No, it's because no one ever told her no including me, but that's changing."

"Surely you two can come to an agreement."

"What? Shared custody? No. I've got to go. I need to circle the wagons. The only person that matters right now is Tommy." She hung up and collapsed into Thomas. "I'm so sorry. This is a total repeat of what happened to you. You can walk away if you want. I'd understand."

He rose from the couch as if that was exactly what he was going to do. Instead, he laid Tommy down in the playpen and came back to her. In seconds, she was in his lap and the safety of his arms.

"It's going to be okay."

"I'm so sorry."

He leaned back to look at her. "This isn't your fault."

She took in a shaky breath. The tears that had been absent before now flowed down her cheeks. "But I'm putting you through the same thing. It's like nightmare on repeat for you."

With a soft caress, he moved her hair from her face. "No, it's not. I thought so too initially, but it's nothing like what happened before."

She sat up taller. "How can you say that? You have a child in your life and it's most likely going to be ripped out of your existence. Do you think you'll see Tommy again when she gets him back?"

He gave her a dark look. "She's not getting him back."

"You're right." She tried to hop off his lap, but he held her to him. "She can't have him if she can't find him. I have to leave."

"No, you'll stay, and you'll fight with me." He looked at the baby. "He's worth fighting for, don't you think?"

"Yes, and he's worth running for too."

"If you took him from me that would be a different scenario."

She leaned into him and let him comfort her. "But you'd still lose him either way."

"Yes, but there's no deceit on your part. You told the truth from the beginning."

"I told you she wouldn't come after the baby and she has."

"You didn't know that. Sarah knew Heather wasn't mine from the beginning. She lied. You were simply mistaken. Heather was never mine. Even if I'd stayed like Sarah wanted me to, she would have never been mine. I wouldn't have been able to trust anything about my life again. It would have been a life built around lies."

"Tommy is not yours either."

He smiled. "Oh, but he is. You brought him to me. You invited me into your lives, and you gave me a son. Named him after me. He's mine. You're mine. I'll fight for both of you."

"Where do we begin?"

"By calling in sick."

They both called off their shifts.

Tommy woke up and Eden fed, bathed and dressed him because Thomas told her to be ready at ten. She stood by the door, her entire being tense and tight as a piano string.

"Hungry?"

"No, I can't eat."

"You'll have to because you can't feed Tommy if you don't. We're going to the diner."

He was right. The damn man was always right, but the diner? At a time like this?

"Shouldn't we be calling someone? I don't have much money, but maybe I can make payments to a lawyer." She held up the summons. "I'm due in court next week. She knows I can't fight her so why draw it out? No doubt she paid extra to expedite the matter. I have a week to make a plan."

He opened the door. "I made a few calls, turns out we have a resident lawyer. Never see him because he spends most of his time commuting to and from his office in Silver Springs. We're meeting Frank at the diner. Turns out he's on vacation."

She walked out, carrying the baby in the safety seat. "Not going to be much of a vacation if he's going to help us."

Thomas helped them into the truck. Before he closed the door, he leaned in and kissed her. "We've got to believe that things will go our way."

Eden didn't like to lie to herself, but hadn't she been doing that her whole life? Especially when it came to her sister? She'd truly believed that Suzanne could do anything she set out to do. She'd never considered the baby was a way to save her marriage. What the hell was she thinking when she agreed to be surrogate for her sister?

"I always wanted her to like me. Wanted to be able to be something special in her eyes. She ignored me my whole life."

Thomas backed out of the driveway and headed toward town. He reached for her hand. "Sometimes we put our faith in the wrong people."

"I had a baby for her so she would value me. What the hell was I thinking?" The truth hurt. She was thinking of herself. Always trying to find her place in her sister's heart.

"Don't beat yourself up. You may have entered into parenthood for a different reason, but it doesn't take away from the fact that you're a good person and a wonderful mother. Maybe this was what the universe wanted for both of us." He squeezed her hand. "It's not how I would have chosen to meet you, but so far it's worked out nicely."

"We're a house of cards ready to fall."

"I can't believe that." He took a quick glance over his shoulder to Tommy, who was again fast asleep, completely unaware of the impact he'd made on so many lives. "Look at him. He's the glue. No way are we falling apart."

They pulled into an open spot in front of

Maisey's Diner and walked inside to find only one man dressed like a lawyer. They had a look to them. Put together, somewhat sinister, expensive.

"Frank?" Thomas laughed. "You're Frank the lawyer?"

"Thomas. You're who called me?"

The two men embraced.

Eden didn't know what the hell was going on. She set Tommy's carrier on the chair next to her and stared at the two men, who seemed to know each other. It wasn't until she cleared her throat that they turned to her.

"You know each other?"

Frank seemed to blush. "Kind of. We played poker in Silver Springs once a month, but then this guy disappeared. Haven't seen him since. We only use first names in the games. Keep it simple. Beer. Poker. Money. What the hell happened to you?"

"It's a long story." He turned to Eden. "He funded that leather sofa we watch Netflix on each night."

"Man's a shark when it comes to card games," Frank said.

Maisey moved toward them with a pot of coffee swinging between her fingers. "You guys want coffee or something?"

"Cakes and bacon for me and Thomas, and

whatever Mr. Arden wants." Eden took the seat next to the baby. Thomas sat on his other side, both of them like sentries guarding a treasure. Frank took the remaining chair and ordered coffee and pie.

He pulled out a yellow legal pad and a pen. "Let's get started."

They sat for an hour and explained the scenario to Frank. He stayed quiet and scribbled notes on a pad of paper. He picked up the summons several times.

"This is just a motion to be heard at this point. We may be able to settle this out of court." He turned to Eden. "Did you say your sister is concerned about public appearances?"

"Yes, it's not who she is but how she's seen that matters."

He smiled. "Great, that will play nicely into our hands."

Eden tore her napkin into tiny shreds. "Will you take payments? I'm working, but it's only part-time."

Thomas turned toward her. "We'll figure it out. I can take a loan."

Frank laughed. "You owe me. We'll settle the cost later. I'm thinking a single game. You win we're pat. You lose and you have to teach me how in the hell you win."

"Basically, you're not charging us?" Eden dunked Thomas's fully intact napkin into her ice water and patted her face. The nerves were eating her alive. Hormone fluctuations and imminent disaster were a bad mix.

He lifted his shoulders. "It's an Aspen Cove thing."

"What's next?" Thomas asked.

"You take care of that baby and leave the rest to me. I'll meet you in court next week. Hopefully, we can clear this up quickly. It's an unusual case and could set a precedent. The best thing for us is to come to an arrangement. If it comes down to a legal custody fight, it's going to be a tough one. I've got some research to do." He gathered his things and left.

"Do you think he's the right fit for the job?" Eden cradled her head in her hands.

"I have to trust Doc. He told me to call him." He looked at her with such love in his eyes. "Doc hasn't led me astray yet."

CHAPTER TWENTY-FIVE

THOMAS

Each day was endless waiting for the court date to appear and then again it seemed to approach at breakneck speed. He didn't understand how something can be both too fast and too slow at the same time.

Going to work was like walking into hell. The job he loved became a heavy burden on his back. Each hour he was at work was an hour he wasn't with Tommy and Eden.

The mornings weren't so much a problem because he could pop over to the vet clinic to see them. He met them for lunch each day, but how was he supposed to shove a lifetime into a week?

Frank and he had shared several conversations and the news was often grim. There were very few cases like theirs. Usually at least one parent shared DNA with the child. That parent was generally awarded custody unless they were deemed unfit. In their case, Tommy wasn't related by genetics to either party, which made the case come down to something as simple as who'd paid for him.

He kept that information from Eden because she wasn't handling the situation well. Her bag was packed and ready to go if she had to run. She didn't know he'd found it, but it was hard to miss her things thinning in the closet they shared.

At a time when they should be rejoicing and looking forward to a life they would share together, they had to worry about keeping all the fragments in one place, so once this was over, they could piece their world back together.

"You ready?" He tugged at the tie at his neck. He didn't normally wear a suit, but he wanted the judge to see him as a man capable of caring for the baby. He knew Brady and Suzanne would be dressed to impress.

"You don't have to come." She smoothed down the front of her dress. Eden was slimming down naturally from breastfeeding but the stress of the impending court case had her dropping weight quickly. She'd lost at least five pounds in the last week.

"I do, and I want to."

"I'm so sorry I got you involved in all this."
She leaned into him and breathed him in. She'd
been doing that a lot. It was as if she was inhaling
him into her memory.

"You didn't. Doc did, and I'm not sorry. You
and the baby are the best things that have happened to me."

"I know but what happens if they take him
away?"

He wrapped her into his arms. "We'll figure
that out if and when we get there."

"How are you so calm?"

He wasn't calm. He was a raging inferno inside but letting it go wouldn't serve anyone. He'd
work his frustration out on the punching bag at
the station tonight.

"I'm trying to be strong for both of us. Let's go
and show them we are the best parents for
Tommy."

FRANK ARDEN MET them at the entrance to
the courthouse.

"Are you two okay?"

Thomas held the baby carrier because Eden's
hands shook so much, he was afraid she'd
drop him.

"We're hanging in there. Aren't we, sweet-heart?" He wanted so badly to kiss the quiver from her lip.

"We're meeting in a smaller courtroom. The Cornings have agreed to let the judge decide the case once everything is laid out."

"Now they're the Cornings?" Eden's voice was razor sharp.

"Better to distance the emotional connection. Trust me, it's best this way."

"Let's get this started so we can get home and resume our lives." Thomas hoped and prayed that this would all be over today, but his gut told him differently. They weren't fighting over a car or a house or a puppy. These proceedings would determine how the lives of five people would play out for eternity. The most important being Tommy.

The clickety-clack of their heels echoed through the halls of the mostly empty courthouse. It was either a slow day for Silver Springs or the Cornings, trying to avoid a public scandal, had managed to finagle their way onto a custom docket.

When Frank Arden opened the door, Thomas saw Eden's sister for the first time. They were nothing alike. Eden was soft and kind looking while Suzanne looked like a fireball spit from a dragon's mouth.

Her expression showed nothing. She had a better poker face than anyone he'd ever met. That was his superpower. It was why he'd won so many games against Frank. He didn't have a tell, but neither did Suzanne. Brady, on the other hand, looked like he'd eaten a green watermelon.

Suzanne moved past her lawyer and rushed toward Eden and the baby until Thomas put the wall of his body between them.

"I'd suggest you move back to your side until the judge grants you permission."

"I want to see my son." She peeked around his body to the carrier he held firmly behind him.

"You can see him if the judge awards you custody. Until then, he's Eden's son, and they belong to me."

She rolled her eyes when she stepped back. "Caveman much?"

The gavel hitting the desk grabbed their attention.

"I'm Judge Russell and I'll be hearing your case." He was a tall man with a head of black hair and a robe to match. "It's my understanding that you'd prefer to avoid a legal battle and would favor a mediation of sorts. This isn't generally how we do business but given the circumstances, I'm willing to try, but I reserve the right to move this to normal court proceedings if that seems necessary. All in agreement?"

They nodded and took seats in front of the desk. The Cornings sat on the right with their lawyer while Eden, Thomas, and Tommy sat on the left with theirs.

It took several hours for both lawyers to state the facts as they knew them. It was the discrepancies in the two stories that had Thomas worried. He knew Eden to be an honest woman, but her sister claimed she'd taken off and wouldn't return her calls. Basically, she accused her of kidnapping.

"I want to get a few things clear." The judge flipped a page of his notepad and started scribbling again. "Eden, you say your sister told you to put the baby up for adoption?"

"She did. She informed me that she and her husband had split, and she no longer wanted the baby."

"Liar," Suzanne called. It took a warning look from her lawyer to shut her up. When she calmed down, she added, "I handed her a check for the delivery and told her I'd be there."

Eden fisted her hands so hard Thomas was certain her nails would draw blood. "Sir, can I say something?" She flexed her hands as if trying to get the blood moving through them again.

"Yes." He turned toward Suzanne and put his finger to his lips.

"I've made a lot of mistakes. I've done many things for the wrong reasons. I had a baby for my sister because I wanted her to value me—to make me a part of her life. She begged me to have a child for her. I've never known her to not put one hundred percent into something she wanted badly. Suzanne always gets what she wants. However, this time she didn't really want the baby. She wanted to hang on to her husband and, like many desperate people, she thought a baby would do it. While I refuse to spread my sister's dirty laundry around in a court of law, her motives were not geared to the child but to her own desires. I'm guilty of that to a point too, but I gave birth to a beautiful boy. I decided to have him for much the same reason as Suzanne. I wanted to keep someone I loved in my life."

"Hard lessons in life are often painful." His pen moved across the page.

"Yes, but they are also the most valuable. I learned a lot about myself along the way. I'm willing to do anything for Tommy. He's the only reason for anything at this point. His existence shows me there's good in the world and perfection in imperfect moments. He reminds me each day that the sunshine doesn't come from the sky, but from his first smile. Each time he grips my hand, he grips my heart. I can appreciate those things, but I'm not sure my sister can. She wants what she wants, but does she know why? I believe you'll make the best decision in the interests of Tommy." She cleared the frog from her throat. "At least I hope you will."

He laid his pen down.

"Ms. Webster. I can see that you love the child, but I also see that you will struggle to provide for him." He looked down at his notes. "You work part time at a vet clinic. You're single and live in a house with a man you've known for a couple of months. Your baby has no room of his own. How is that providing a stable life for him?"

Thomas wanted to shout out that he wasn't just a man who shared a house with her. He was financially able to support them both, but he was not part of the suit and had been warned by Frank to not speak.

"You're right. I live with a man who has been a father to Thomas. Who pays the mortgage on time and provides everything we need. I live in a town that seems to know what I need before I do. I only have to think about it, and it seems to show up on the front porch. It's not conventional, but it's perfect in its own way. What's better for Tommy? Should he be surrounded by people who have wanted him from the beginning or handed off to a woman who wanted to return her purchase?" Eden pulled out the uncashed check. "I never cashed it because how could a value be put on his life?" She reached into the carrier and picked up the baby. "Tommy can't be bought, but he can be loved. Who is better suited to do that? Me, who has shown that I'll do anything for him, or my sister who will turn him over to capable hands until he can go to boarding school?"

"I'd never," Suzanne screamed. "He's mine. I paid for him. Picked out everything about him. He's perfect because of me."

Brady shook his head and leaned back like he'd given up. Suzanne's lawyer asked her to take a seat, which she reluctantly did but probably only because her stilettos were killing her feet.

"You see," Eden said. "She buys what she wants, and she's angry because for the first time in her life someone is pushing back." She turned toward her sister. "Odd that it would be me, right?" She hugged Tommy to her chest. "He's worth the fight."

Thomas was never so proud to be in her presence. He knew she was filled with rage and worry, but she talked calmly and from the heart. She said all the things he was thinking and couldn't say. He knew without a doubt he loved her.

The judge rose, as did everyone else. "I'd like to take a recess and resume this tomorrow." He looked at his schedule. "I've got an opening at three."

Thomas was concerned about several things that had come out in the hearing today. Things he would put to rest right away. First, he needed Eden out of the house and occupied so he could call in some favors.

She was right when she said it was time to circle the wagons.

Once they were in the truck, he turned to her. "It's going to be okay."

"In whose world? You heard him. 'You have a part-time job. No permanent place to stay. No room for your child. No money.' He's going to give the baby to them."

"No. I won't let that happen."

He pulled onto the highway. "You're staying at the bed and breakfast tonight. Sage's guests have cleared out and I think it's best if you don't stay alone while I'm on shift."

She knew he was right because she didn't argue or maybe she'd given up completely and had no fight left in her.

It didn't matter because he had enough fight left in him for both of them.

CHAPTER TWENTY-SIX

EDEN

"Tea?" Sage asked. "I'd offer to cook you something, but I fear I'd kill you trying."

"Tea would be great. Decaf if you have it. It's better for the baby." She hadn't put Tommy down since Thomas had dropped her off. She was so afraid that she'd have to hand him over tomorrow that she needed to memorize the weight of him in her arms. The smell of his baby fresh hair. The feel of his velvet soft skin.

"Cannon is going to stop at Dalton's and get something for dinner. The girls will be over soon. I thought a baby fest would be great. Marina will bring hers along in utero since the little bugger doesn't want to come out. He's a week late and Doc is threatening to induce. Katie will bring over Sahara which will make you second guess having children altogether. Why do they morph from angels to demons?" She walked to the kitchen and returned moments later with a cup of hot water and a tea bag. "Charlie ... that woman thought having two at once would be wise."

Despite the somber situation, Eden giggled because she'd seen how harried Charlie could get. "She came to work in her slippers the other day. At least they matched because last week she had on two different shoes."

"Trig is a huge help, but I can't imagine having a baby need me so much."

Eden looked down at Tommy. "Hold him while I make my tea?" She didn't wait for an answer. She placed her baby in Sage's arms. "I thought you and Cannon were going to try."

"Oh, we're trying all right. They say practice makes perfect but jeez didn't you hear me? I can't even cook a meal. Kids want stuff like pancakes and pretty little crust-free sandwiches."

She sipped the warm tea and relished the soothing feeling of it going down. Each heated sip released some of the tension of the day.

"No, all they want is to be loved. You would do that. I see that in everything you do, from the way you helped deliver Tommy to the way you look at your husband. All the other stuff is just stuff."

Sage held the baby against her and rocked. She was a natural, but then again, she was originally a labor and delivery nurse.

When Sage frowned, Eden braced herself for the question she knew was coming.

"What if they take him away?"

She swallowed a lump the size of a boulder. "I have to believe they won't, but if they do, I'll figure out a way to survive. This was always supposed to be the way of it. I was having a baby for my sister. If that's the way it pans out, then the original goal takes precedence."

"You make it sound like it's easy, but I know you're putting on a brave face. Do you think Suzanne will be a bad parent?"

She thought about that. "No, I think she'll do the best she can do. No one goes into parenting thinking they'll be bad, but I imagine we all have days we're not proud of. The trick is to do better the next time. I think Suzanne will be the best parent she can be, and she'll fill in the gaps with others that can provide what she can't."

The front door opened and in ran Sahara. Her pigtails bobbed with each unsteady step she took.

"Baby," she called out and raced toward Sage.

Katie laughed. "She's been crawling the walls

to get here. I caught her sneaking out the back door twice. Didn't think I'd need to worry about her sneaking out for boys for at least another decade."

Eden picked up Sahara and turned her around to face her. "You want to hold him?" The little imp nodded. "Maybe if you ask your Aunt Sage nicely, she'll help you."

Sage moved to the couch. As soon as she was situated, Eden put Sahara down. The little girl sidled up to Sage in no time and half cradled Tommy, who woke up but was happy with the attention he was getting.

"You hanging in there?" Katie put a tray of sweets on the table. "This is my go-to when I'm down, stressed, PMS, angry, happy. Oh hell, I just love sweets. Who needs an excuse?"

"I'm falling apart on the inside but trying to hold it together on the outside."

Katie pulled her in for a hug. "I remember a scared woman who could have written any wish she wanted on a yellow sticky but only wished that everything would turn out right for her child. You've got a lot of wish makers in your midst. Let's see what kind of magic we can pull together." She picked up a cranberry orange muffin. "Let's start with this."

A clatter at the door had Katie running to help

Charlie in with her double stroller. "I swear this is more trouble than it's worth. I need a backpack that can hold one baby on the front and the other on the back and I can twist it around with ease to care for them both."

"Or you can learn to drive your stroller," Marina said from behind her.

"Or that?" Charlie walked in pushing the babies in front of her. Through all the racket they remained asleep.

Sahara lost interest in Tommy and ran for the twins. "Babies," she hollered, but the little ones didn't stir.

"How is that possible?" Eden asked. "They sleep through anything."

"They take after Daddy. Besides, we followed the sage advice to live our lives normally. We're noisy, and they've adjusted." Charlie parked the stroller next to the plaid chair she kicked Otis out of and collapsed. "I'm exhausted." She leaned forward and looked at the plate of sweets. "Is that a brownie?"

"It's yours."

"You eat chocolate?"

Charlie laughed. "Only if I'm mad at Trig, and it's his night to get up with the boys." She grinned devilishly and snatched a brownie. "The man had the nerve to ask me if I ever wanted a girl."

Everyone laughed. "Not thinking with the head on his shoulders."

"He's a man," Sage said.

Marina took up the other plaid chair while her daughter Kellyn joined Sahara ogling the babies. She'd heard Marina's story and held a huge amount of respect for a woman who put the interests of a child before her own. The abuse she'd taken to protect Kellyn had to be like living in hell. If Marina could make it past that and come out on the right side, Eden had to hope that she'd do the same. At the end of the day, all she cared about was Tommy and that he was in the best place possible for him. In her heart, she knew where that was, but she hoped Judge Russell agreed.

"Tell me, Eden. How did you go into labor? I've tried everything. Was it sex? They say it can push you into labor, but my damn husband won't play along. He thinks the baby should come when it's ready. I'm ready. Doesn't that account for something?"

Eden shook her head. "I haven't had sex in almost two years."

The room went silent. She had imagined everyone knew her story by now. It was no secret she was a surrogate situation gone wrong or actually in this case gone right.

"None? Like no sex?" Sage handed Tommy to her and picked up a cookie. "You and Thomas haven't?"

"No, I'm just coming up on the six weeks and honestly, I didn't know him well enough to have sex before. Not that I would have. I was pregnant and huge and unattractive." She bit her lips after the words came out. Turning to Marina, she grimaced. "Sorry, I wasn't inferring that pregnant women weren't sexy. I never felt sexy in the last stage. I was big and cumbersome, but that's just me. I didn't mean to offend."

"No offense taken. I don't want Aiden because I want him sexually, I need him or what he can bring to the sheets. I swear I've been pregnant for forty-two weeks."

"You haven't. You miscalculated and you were actually less pregnant than we thought. You're in week forty now."

"That's your story but I tell you when he comes out, I'm forever going to call him my tenth month baby."

Eden warmed. "It's a boy? What will you name him?"

"We don't know. We want to see him first."

Sage swallowed her cookie. "Let's get back to

sex." She pointed at Marina. "The baby will come when he's ready." She pointed to Eden. "You're good to go when you're ready."

"Really?"

"Take it slow. It's a bit pinchy the first time after, but then it's fine," Sage advised.

Katie sang out a loud rendition of "Like a Virgin," just as Louise Williams walked in with two large takeout containers.

"I've got food."

"I thought Cannon was bringing something from Dalton's," Eden asked. There was a lot going on in the house. It was as if they were all keeping her occupied for other reasons than only easing her worried mind.

"The boys are busy tonight."

"What are you up to?"

"Nothing." They all flashed her innocent smiles. "Just doing what we do best."

CHAPTER TWENTY-SEVEN

THOMAS

Thomas was bone tired. He'd worked all night long with the help of his friends to make sure that no stone was left unturned when it came to Eden and Tommy. If they lost the war it wouldn't be because they weren't fit for battle.

He looked around at what used to be his man cave. Where his big screen used to hang on the wall now held the hand carved wooden animals shaped into letters that spelled Tommy. Cannon had whittled away at them all night. The walls were painted a soft bluish gray to match Tommy's eyes. Poor Bowie was left with more paint on him than he'd put on the walls.

Mark Bancroft had enlisted the help of his photographer wife Poppy to lighten the place up with pictures she'd taken around town. The people who would impact Tommy's life hung on the walls. Dalton supplied the food they needed to get through the long night.

Even Doc stayed up until he couldn't keep his shaggy brows from sagging. He mostly supervised and told the men how proud he was that everyone was pitching in.

Wes Covington, the local builder, whipped up a few pieces of furniture like a changing table and a toy chest. He also helped Thomas put together a crib he'd run to Copper Creek to buy. Luke took his shift, so the town was covered while they tried to make a little magic.

In his gut, he knew it would come down to what you had, not what the baby needed. They couldn't compete financially, but he was damned if he'd let Eden stand up there and not be able to prove she could care for the baby. She was the right choice.

Dressed in his uniform so Eden wouldn't know what he'd been up to all night, he walked to the bed and breakfast to pick her up for their next court appointment. He debated on telling her, but he didn't want to get her hopes up only to be dashed. Couldn't imagine coming back to the house without Tommy and seeing the room. No, if that happened, he'd lock the room up until he could dismantle it. No use bringing her more pain than she was already drowning in.

He didn't need to knock. The door opened and she flew into his arms.

"I missed you so much."

He held her and breathed her in. "I missed you too." He stepped back and looked at her shadowy eyes. The dark circles were a testament to how much sleep she'd missed from worry. "It's going to be okay."

"No, it's not, but we can't control what happens to us, only how we react to it. This is real life and it's messy. How am I supposed to say goodbye if she wins?"

"Hold on tight, Eden. It's not time for goodbye." He pulled her to the steps and sat on the top, then patted the space beside him. "Where's Tommy? Can you spend a minute with me?"

"Sage is fawning over him. I think she's got the bug again."

He chuckled. "That would make Cannon happy. He's dying to whittle away for his own child." He thought about the detail he'd put into each piece for Tommy and knew that Cannon's child's room would be filled with his dad's creative love.

She cupped his cheek. "You look tired. Was it a tough night?"

275

She tilted her head. Despite the uncertainness of the day, one look in her eyes and he knew without a doubt he loved her.

"You okay?" She thumbed at the dark rings under his eyes. He had a look of a prizefighter when he glanced in the mirror. Bruised markings from a fight with worry and exhaustion.

"Yes." He took a deep breath. "Before we go, I need you to know something."

She went to speak and he brushed her lip with his thumb.

"No matter what happens you need to know that you've changed my life."

"You've changed mine too. Thank you for all you've done. I know I've been a burden, and yet you've never complained."

"No, you haven't. You were a shock and a surprise and exactly what I didn't think I needed, and yet, you were everything I did. I love Tommy. How can I not? But he's not the reason I want to talk to you. You are." He took a fortifying breath because he never thought he'd utter these words to another woman in his life outside of his mother and yet they were so easy to say to Eden. "I love you. I'm so damn in love with you my insides ache from it. No matter how this goes down today, I'm going to be here for you. You and I will work it out together."

She let her forehead fall into his chest. "God, why does love have to be so hard?"

He froze. Was she telling him she didn't feel the same way?

When she looked up at him with all the love he felt showing in her eyes he breathed a sigh of relief. "Sometimes the things we have to fight for are worth more. I'm fighting for you. For Tommy. For me. For us."

Her smile brightened the moment. "I'm so glad you scooped me off the ground. My life without you in it is less. I love you too." She opened her mouth like she was going to speak but stopped.

"Shall we claim our son?"

"He'll be happy to see his father."

It was funny how they hadn't talked about long-term until that moment and yet the whole time they talked about parenting their child. Tommy was a gift to the world that they were allowed to experience.

They rose to their feet and went inside the bed and breakfast.

Sage rushed over and placed the swaddled baby boy into his arms. Everything felt perfect for the moment. He cooed at him and smiled and made silly baby noises and didn't care how ridiculous he might look. All that mattered was that Tommy smiled back. Doc tried to tell him a smile this early was merely gas, but Thomas knew better. Tommy felt loved and it showed in his happy face.

Almost an hour later, they walked up the steps to the courthouse. The halls were busy, and he wished for the more laid-back atmosphere of yesterday. With all the suits moving through the corridors it became real in a way that hit him harder than before.

Frank Arden saw them walking toward Judge Russell's small courtroom.

"We're in the same room. It's usually used for small disputes."

Thomas's eyes lifted. "There's nothing small about the custody of a child."

"I understand, but the atmosphere is better for everyone involved. Small intimate rooms make people feel less threatened."

"We feel threatened enough."

Frank opened the door to let Eden and the

baby through. He stopped Thomas on the threshold. "I think what you did last night will help. I got your list of questions to ask. Thank you. I didn't think we'd need to go at them from this angle, but you may be right."

"Over the years I've gotten good at reading people." Thomas had to thank Sarah for that. Since her betrayal he analyzed people. He watched for changes in their mannerisms. Yesterday's day in court gave him a lot to evaluate. Suzanne was not mother material. Her pleas to see her son might have twisted a lesser man's heartstrings, but what came out of her mouth never showed up in her eyes. The same could be said of Sarah.

Off to the right sat Suzanne and Brady. Her expression was as pinched as his was bored.

When the judge walked into the room everyone rose. Including most of the town of Aspen Cove, who were seated in the back waiting for their turn to be called on if needed. The door flew open and Sage rushed in to take a seat beside her sister Lydia.

"We have a crowd here today." Judge Russel eyed the visitors and frowned. "Shall we get started?"

"Your honor," started Frank, "you asked a lot of questions of Eden yesterday but none of Mrs.

Corning. As this is a court of law and law is based on the tilting of scales in favor of one person or the other, isn't it fair that the same questions be asked?"

"Counselor Arden, the only thing in question here is who is better equipped to care for the child. I spent some time on this last night. We can't decide based on DNA. The child belongs genetically to an egg donor and a sperm donor who wish to remain anonymous. It puts the court in an awkward position because then it comes down to who owned the ovum which would no doubt be the Cornings since they have the documentation to prove it."

He thumbed through his notes and shook his head.

"Ms. Webster, why would you give birth to a child for another woman when you haven't had one for yourself? It's quite unusual and not recommended from everything I researched."

Eden stood holding the baby to her chest. "It's simple. I loved my sister more than I loved myself. My loyalties might have been misplaced, but they were honest."

"Your honor," Frank said. "Will you at least give our questions a look before you decide the fate of Tommy Webster?"

Thomas couldn't wait to make Eden his wife

and give them both his last name. Eden and Tommy Cross had a ring to it.

The judge huffed. "Bring them here."

Frank rushed the list of questions to the judge and then stood beside Eden. Thomas could hear her question him about what was on the paper.

Frank replied loud enough for him to hear. "Just simple things that your sister should have to answer. You did or at least you will." He turned toward the people who had come out to support them. "They are here for you too."

It killed him to be separated from her. She was drowning by herself. He could see her knees shake and her lip twitch. He couldn't stand it any longer. He raised his hand. "Your honor. Can I join Eden so she has support?"

The judge shook his head then nodded.

Thomas rushed to her while the judge poured over the questions.

It was the longest minute of his life, but he kept hold of Eden and the baby and waited for the judge to decide.

"I came in here today thinking it was an open and shut case. The Cornings paid for an ovum and found a host in Ms. Webster. She went into the job open eyed and knowing that at the end of the term she would relinquish the child." He paused for a few minutes. "By all rights the Cornings should be the legal guardians of the child currently named Tommy."

Suzanne turned to them and smiled. She thought she'd won.

It never occurred to Thomas that if they lost him, everything about Tommy would change, including his name.

"However, I did come with a few questions myself because something about Mrs. Corning's last-minute change of heart doesn't sit right with me." He stared straight at her. His look was hard and penetrating. "What would have happened if your sister had done as you asked and put the baby up for adoption?"

Suzanne stood and held her head high. "I would have searched the ends of the earth for him." She sounded convincing.

"Maybe, but that's not how parenthood works. You don't get to buy it and return it when it doesn't fit. I do feel a few questions posed to both of you would help me decide." He removed his glasses and cleaned them on his black robe. "First to the Cornings. Do you have a room set up for Tommy?"

"Well," Suzanne said. "We've hired an interior designer to start on one as soon as we get word that Tommy is ours."

"Okay." The judge was stone-faced. "And you, Ms. Webster?"

"Oh, um well..."

Thomas broke in and pulled a handful of photos from his shirt pocket. "Your honor, I took these this morning. This is Tommy's room." He fanned them out in front of Eden before he handed them to Frank to give to the judge.

"Oh, my God," Eden whispered. "That's what you were all up to?"

"Yes."

She swiped the tears from her eyes and leaned into him. "I love you."

The judge moved through the photos and smiled. "Love the letters. Know where I can get them? I've got a grandchild on the way."

"Yes, sir," Thomas said. "Cannon Bishop makes them." He turned and pointed to his friend, who lifted his hand and smiled.

"What about a doctor? Mrs. Corning, have you set up a pediatrician? Children need immunizations and check-ups."

"Um ... we have one in mind."

The judge looked at Eden. "And you?"

A broad smile spread across her face because she knew where this was heading. "Tommy has two doctors. He was delivered by Doc Parker and he is also seen by Doctor Lydia Covington. He has a lovely nurse named Sage Bishop who worked for years in labor and delivery." She turned and they stood and waved.

"I see." He went through his list of questions and each time Eden had a solid answer and person sitting behind her willing to step up to the plate. Suzanne couldn't say the same. Even her husband had started to grumble and tell her to give it up.

"One final thing." He looked at Eden. "Bear with me for a moment. Can you please walk Tommy over to your sister so she can hold him?"

Eden gave him a feral look. The kind a lioness gives when her cub might be in danger.

"Humor me, Ms. Webster."

Eden walked Tommy to her sister and placed him in her hands. Suzanne held him out with her arms stretched far in front of her as if to avoid being infected.

"If I were to grant you custody today, are you prepared to take this child home and love him like you gave birth to him?"

The look on Suzanne's face was priceless. "Well, no. You asked the questions. His room isn't ready. I have nothing prepared to take care of a child. Surely my sister can keep him until we're ready."

The judge laughed. "That's what I thought. The way I see it, Mrs. Corning, is that you had over nine months to prepare for the birth of your child. You never wanted a child, just loved the idea of having one. You can't buy a baby like you do a purse. I don't know who's nuttier in this case. You for wanting a baby or your sister for wanting to give you one." His dark hair shone like obsidian under the overhead lights. "Take your child back, Ms. Webster. Take him home and love him like you have been. He's in good hands." The gavel hit its mark on the desk and the crowd erupted into cheers.

"He's mine?" Eden took him from her sister, but she didn't gloat. "Suzanne, I'm sorry. Maybe someday when you're ready. When I'm ready. We can talk about this. He's a wonderful little boy who wouldn't have come into this world without you."

Her sister watched as she cradled Tommy and gave her a half smile. "You know how I hate to lose."

She moved closer. "Look at him. How can any of us consider ourselves losers?" She walked away.

Thomas embraced them both and held on tightly. "I was going to tell the judge I'd marry you on the spot if that was what he needed."

"I don't know where you came from."

"Hell, baby, I came straight out of the pits of

hell and landed in your heaven. Shall we go home and show our boy his room?"

They walked out hand in hand. "No wonder you're so tired."

"I'm exhausted."

She sidled into him. "You know ... I was told I'm good to go."

"Good to go?" He stopped and cocked his head.

"Yes, as in ... you know ... healed. I thought maybe since we had a child together it might be time to make love."

"All of a sudden, I'm not that tired."

CHAPTER TWENTY-EIGHT

EDEN

Eden stood for far too long in Tommy's room staring at all the town had done for them. She tucked his little blanket up over his shoulders and gave him a pat. Tonight would be the first time he'd sleep away from her.

How would she have given him to her sister when she couldn't walk down the hallway to be seconds from him? The only thing that kept her moving away was Thomas, who was waiting for her in their bedroom.

When she walked inside, he was already in bed, the sheet only covering his lower body. God was he beautiful. He'd always been respectful with her. Short of seeing him once in a towel, he never slept out of his shorts and T-shirt. He said it was his uniform. If he got the call about a fire at night, all he'd need to do was jump into his gear.

"Is he down?"

She moved toward him. "Yes, he's had quite a busy day. I think he'll sleep for hours." She sat on the edge of the bed, but he grabbed her and pulled her to him.

"Good, because I'll need hours." He tugged her shirt over her head and stared at her. His fingertips caressed the exposed flesh of her breasts. "I've hoped for this moment for a long time."

"Really? Since when?"

"Since that first day when I saw you from behind in the store. Baby, your body was perfection."

"I was eight months pregnant."

"Yes, with my son and I didn't even know it." He reached around to unclasp her bra. Her full breasts fell into his hands. He laid her back and leaned over her, kissing her with the same love and passion she had for him. They'd quite excelled at kissing since they'd been practicing for months. She loved it when he nibbled on her bottom lip. Couldn't get enough of his velvet soft tongue against hers. He tasted like sweetness and sex and forever.

It didn't take long for him to strip her down to nothing. She didn't have anything to hide. He'd seen it all and came back for more.

His hand rested on her soft tummy.

"Kind of gross," Eden said.

"Kind of awesome." He kissed her from her belly button down to the single stretchmark that marred her lower stomach. "We can wait. Tonight, we can just rejoice in our good fortune. It doesn't have to be this."

She tugged off the sheet that was still wrapped around his hips. "Thomas Cross, I've been waiting for you all my damn life. Now make love to me." She reached down to grip his length and inhaled. "But be gentle. I hear it's pinchy at first."

He lined himself up and entered her slowly. It pinched for only a second, and then it was pure bliss. His body moved inside hers like a symphony. Each stroke hitting the perfect note. Sex with someone she loved was different. It was more than feeling good. It started in her heart and ended with her core quivering around him. While the climax was amazing, the connection was what she'd feel for the rest of her life.

Thomas was everything she didn't know she needed. When he moved inside her, he was everything she could never live without. They made love over and over again until Tommy woke up hungry. She fed him, and they made love again.

She'd never get enough of this man who'd rescued her and in turn seemed to rescue himself. As they lay sated and exhausted after a night of perfection, she rolled into him.

"You gave up your man cave for us. Maybe I can help you work on the spare room if we can get Porkchop to ever leave it."

He chuckled. "Poor cat is damaged for life. She'll never recover from seeing Tom in a tuxedo but maybe we can coax her out of the room."

"We can start on that soon if you want. I don't want you to be without."

"You think I'm ever going to be without with you and Tommy in my life?" She laughed. "We'll fix up the room, but it won't be a man cave. I gave the sofa to Tilden Cool and the big screen to Peter. The man is almost blind. Although he sees more than he lets on. He saw early on that you were right for me."

She laid her head on his bare chest. "He's a wise one, but what are we going to do with the spare room?"

"Get it ready for the daughter I'll give you someday."

CHAPTER TWENTY-NINE

EDEN

Two months later.

Thomas and Eden sat at their favorite table. It was the one they'd sat at the first time they ate together—when he'd known the table would be more comfortable than a booth for her. He was always observant in a way her sister never could be. Maybe that came down to maturity or self-awareness or both. How could anyone consider another when they were focused on themselves?

The diner was fairly full, with Doc sitting in his corner booth reading his paper. The Williams family took up several tables with their family of ten. Sheriff Cooper and Marina sat with Kellyn and Logan, who had been born the day Tommy officially became theirs.

A quiet man Thomas called Tilden sat alone by the silent jukebox. She'd always wondered about him. He was like a knot in the wood paneling. Always around but no one really noticed.

Tommy played with the toys hanging from his carrier. He was partial to the stuffed monkeys and giraffes his Aunt Suzanne had sent him.

Today was a big day. Eden's newly single sister was coming for her first visit.

"Are you sure this is a good idea?" Thomas asked. He'd been testy all morning. He was protective of them. Like a caveman who pounded his chest and yelled mine. She loved him for it. He'd proven he'd do anything for them, including giving up his beloved man cave. He had to love her to send his ninety-six-inch, high definition TV across the street to Peter Larkin. He might not like the idea of Suzanne right now, but he'd come around. Thomas always did.

"It's the right thing to do."

"Maybe, but she doesn't deserve it."

"No, you're probably right, but how will she learn if others don't teach her?"

"She's a damn grownup, Eden. Over a decade older than you, and yet, you're so much smarter."

Eden laughed. It was true. There were all kinds of smart. Street smart. Book smart. Love smart. A person could be smart about anything, but they'd never be smart about everything. Her sister was on a steep learning curve to intelligence.

Brady had left her and taken everything with him. Suzanne was back to working a lesser job for lesser pay. She no longer lived in a Breckenridge mansion but a small apartment in Keystone. Her days weren't filled with high-level business meetings and expensive lunches. She got a single property out of the divorce. A small townhome complex that catered to ski bums and summer hippies.

The door to the diner opened and Suzanne walked in, looking so unlike the woman Eden knew. Her hair was pulled into a ponytail. Her face was free of makeup. Her smile was genuine.

She approached slowly as if walking a minefield.

"Hey," she said. "Thanks for meeting me." She took a seat next to Eden and looked at the baby.

"Good to see you, sis." She pulled Tommy out of the carrier. "You want to hold him?"

Thomas let out a growl.

"Down, boy," Suzanne teased. "I'm not here to take your bone."

He lifted a brow. "You wouldn't even get to the door."

Suzanne sighed. "I'm sorry for everything." She looked at the baby again and opened her arms.

"I'm not sorry about him though. He was a gift. My gift to you. Your gift to me. He taught me a lot about myself. Taught me that while you were selfless, I'd been otherwise. I'm working on that."

Eden placed the baby in her arms and watched her sister melt.

"I've been practicing. I volunteer at the hospital and hold preemies for hours and rock them."

"They let you volunteer?" Thomas grumbled. "Around babies?"

"Yes, there's nothing like the feel of another woman's child. At the end of the day, I get to go home and sleep eight hours. My boobs are still where they were years ago, and I can have all the wine I want." She smiled. "This was always the way it should have been." She cooed at Tommy and told him how she would spoil him. "I'll make a better auntie than a mommy."

"Wish you could have come to the wedding," Eden said. She looked down at the simple gold band that meant everything. She and Thomas had tied the knot in front of a big oak tree in Hope Park surrounded by their friends. Doc had married them. It seemed fitting to be married by the man who had brought them together.

"It was the same day as my divorce. A fabulous day, for the records." She looked at Thomas. "By the way, how did you two meet?"

Eden laughed. "He found me on the street and plied me with Good & Plenty."

"That's a new take on finding a mate. I'll have to write that one down."

Just then, the door to the diner opened and a woman dressed in an elaborate white wedding gown rushed in. She looked around the crowd and said, "I need a groom, and I need one now." She stared straight at Tilden. "What about you?"

"Scratch that," Suzanne said. "I like her style." She hugged her nephew to her chest and watched the scene unfold.

Next up is One Hundred Secrets

ALSO BY KELLY COLLINS

An Aspen Cove Romance Series

One Hundred Reasons

One Hundred Heartbeats

One Hundred Wishes

One Hundred Promises

One Hundred Excuses

One Hundred Christmas Kisses

One Hundred Lifetimes

One Hundred Ways

One Hundred Goodbyes

One Hundred Secrets

One Hundred Regrets

One Hundred Choices

One Hundred Decisions

One Hundred Glances

One Hundred Lessons

One Hundred Mistakes

One Hundred Nights

One Hundred Whispers
One Hundred Reflections
One Hundred Intentions
One Hundred Chances
One Hundred Dreams

ABOUT THE AUTHOR

International bestselling author of more than thirty novels, Kelly Collins writes with the intention of keeping love alive. Always a romantic, she blends real-life events with her vivid imagination to create characters and stories that lovers of contemporary romance, new adult, and romantic suspense will return to again and again.

For More Information
www.authorkellycollins.com
kelly@authorkellycollins.com

Made in the USA
Monee, IL
24 June 2023

37167419R00167